MARY

MW01241143

ROBERT AINSLEIGH

VOLUME I

Elibron Classics
www.elibron.com

ASHER'S COLLECTION

OF

ENGLISH AUTHORS

BRITISH AND AMERICAN.

COPYRIGHT EDITION.

VOL. 11.

ROBERT AINSLEIGH BY M. E. BRADDON.

IN THREE VOLUMES.

VOL. I.

ROBERT AINSLEIGH

BY

M. E. BRADDON

AUTHOR OF 'LADY AUDLEY'S SECRET'
ETC. ETC. ETC.

COPYRIGHT EDITION.

IN THREE VOLUMES.

VOL. I.

———

BERLIN
A. ASHER & CO.
1872.

CONTENTS OF VOL. I.

ROBERT AINSLEIGH.

CHAPTER I.

MY FIRST HOME.

My earliest recollections are of a scene which throgh-out an eventful life has been, and to the end of life will remain, in my esteem the brightest region of this various and beautiful world. From Indian forests, from the shores of mightier rivers, under the light of larger stars, my thoughts have flown back to the streams and woods of my early home, and taken shelter there, as young birds return to the nest they have been too eager to abandon.

I was born in London, in the year 1731, but of my birthplace or of those who watched my cradle I have no recollection. My first babyish steps trod the soft turf of a gentleman's park in Berkshire—a domain so

large, that in my childish ideas the world beyond its
boundaries must needs be very narrow. Deep in the
heart of this sylvan scene there was a gamekeeper's
cottage, and to the gamekeeper's honest wife I owed
those maternal cares which transformed a sickly
infant into a sturdy lad.

Until my tenth year this cottage was my only home;
Jack Hawker, the gamekeeper, his wife, and their
little girl Margery, my only friends. Nor did I sigh
for other companionship or a more agreeable abode.
The low plastered cottage, the slanting thatched roof,
pointed gables, and small casement windows, cur-
tained with roses and honeysuckle, appeared to me
the perfection of a dwelling-place. It had been called
the warrener's lodge in the old times, when the skins
of rabbits and conies were employed for the costume
of English knights and squires, and the rabbit-warren
was a feature of great importance in a gentleman's
estate. It still stood on the border of a great warren,
the safe keeping whereof was one of my foster-father's
duties.

This tranquil home I loved with all my heart, and
my little sister Margery—for by that tender name I
had learned to call her—I regarded as the dearest of
created beings. With her I spent my days, wander-

ing hand-in-hand among the fern and underwood,
knowing the progress of time only by the different
wild-flowers which the changing seasons gave us.

Nor did we lack companions and playfellows in our
childish sports. The sylvan depths we inhabited were
alive with wild creatures that had grown almost tame
in this deep solitude. Mild-eyed fawns watched us
gravely while we played ; squirrels leaped and frisked
before us, no more conscious than ourselves of life's
realities ; partridge and pheasant, blackbird and
thrush, fluttered the young fern in the bright days
of early summer ; and in the shadow of a copse that
was purple with hyacinths the rabbits swarmed thick
as Virgil's famous bees.

This was my world from my first hours of infantine
consciousness until my tenth birthday; and bitter was
the stroke which ended this phase of my life. On
the knees of the keeper's wife I had uttered my first
prayer; in the brawny arms of the keeper I had been
carried before I learned to walk. The first syllables
which my lips had shaped were those that called these
good creatures Mammy and Daddy. I was but just
old enough to perceive the progress of events when
little Margery's baby-face first beamed upon our family
circle, and from that hour I had tenderly loved the

fair-haired baby, who grew betimes into my sister and companion.

In those early years of my life I tasted perfect happiness ; and not to the lips of many children is that cup offered. Over the fairest childhood there is generally some shadow—sickness or change of fortune, a cross nurse or a careless mother. But in the humble home where I was reared, there was no skeleton lurking in secret cupboard. The keeper and his wife were young, honest, and healthy. They loved each other fondly, and had affection to spare for the foster-child that came to them before their own. For these good creatures life was not to be all sunshine ; for them, as for me, there were to be trial and tempest and gloom ; but the halcyon days of their existence were these which I shared with them,—a period of calm and pure delight, which was destined to haunt me in many a scene of horror and death, in many an hour of heart-sickness and despondency.

My pleasures in these days were of the simplest. To trudge beside the keeper on his morning round ; once, on a rare occasion of never-to-be-forgotten delight, to watch with him in the moonlit woods for midnight snarers of hare and pheasant ; to ride to the market-town with mammy in a lumbering cart, which

the good soul sometimes drove; to hunt for mush-
rooms in the dewy mornings ; to pick blackberries in
October, and to roast chestnuts with Margery among
the ashes at Christmas,—these were the chief excite-
ments of my childhood.

Neighbours we had none. The nearest village was
seven miles away from us. The nearest habitation
was the great house in the centre of the park ; a
mansion of the Elizabethan era, encircled by a broad
moat, and approached by a grim arched gateway
that belonged to a much earlier period.

The fairy tales which I had heard at this time must
needs have been few ; yet I never beheld this gloomy
gateway, flanked by its twin gothic towers, nor did I
ever peer into the dark still water of the moat, without some vague sense of the supernatural, some
instinctive feeling of awe, which was stronger even
than my curiosity.

The dreary quiet of the place, the long rows of
shuttered casements, the absence of sound or movement on the terraces and in the courts, the massive
towers, and the iron-clamped gates, which seemed no
more likely to be opened than the black doors of the
mausoleum in the park,—were indeed calculated to
inspire unwonted thoughts in the breast of childhood.

When I was old enough to be curious, I questioned my good-humoured daddy, and he freely imparted all he knew about the mansion which filled me with such wonder.

He told me that house and park and woods, and the little church within the park-walls, where there was service on alternate Sundays, all belonged alike to his mistress, Lady Barbara Lestrange, who lived in foreign parts, whither her husband, Sir Marcus Lestrange, had been sent ambassador.

'Which be a kind o' king in its way,' added the keeper, with the pride of a faithful servant, whose master's honours are in some sort his own.

'And does no one live at the great house now, daddy?' I asked.

'No one but old Anthony Grimshaw and his wife, and a couple of women servants. A rare starched gentleman is Tony Grimshaw, and has been house-steward to my lady and my lady's father these thirty years. They do say as Mrs. Grimshaw's a brimstone; but she have always been kind to me and my wife, and 'twould come ill from me to say aught agen her. Madge was housemaid up at the great house afore I married her, in the old earl's time ; and she's owned to me that Mother Grimshaw was a bit of a scold.

She was Martha Peyton then, and own-maid to Lady Barbara, and they say as she must have frightened old Tony into marrying her. But she's been kind to us in the hard winters; and when Sissy was born, she sent us groats and wine and tea, and such-like fal-lals; so we'll let bygones be bygones Robin.'

'And has Lady Barbara been kind to thee, daddy?' I asked. (We "thee'd" and "thou'd" each other in these parts; but I shall take no pains to reproduce the patois of the county, which I have indeed in some part forgotten, having heard and conversed in many strange languages since I first learned my native tongue from honest Jack Hawker, my foster-father.) 'Has she been kind to thee, daddy?' I reiterated.

'Ah, Robin, kind enough in the way of fine folks like her. She brought thee to my wife to nurse, and has paid me handsomely for thy bite and sup.'

This was not the first time I had heard that I was but an alien in the home I loved so dearly.

'She brought me, daddy! Where did she bring me from?'

'From London, Rob; where thou wouldst have starved, poor orphan, but for her. The Lord knows where my lady found thee; but she was ever charitable and kind to the poor. Thou wert the sickliest infant ever these eyes looked upon, and thou must thank my wife Madge that thou art alive to-day.'

'I wish thou wert my real father, daddy,' I said. Whereon sturdy Jack Hawker snatched me up in his great arms and covered me with kisses.

' So do I, little one,' he cried, with an oath ; 'but wishing won't make thee mine ; and some day my lady will come and take thee away from daddy and mammy.'

This set me blubbering, and the good fellow had hard work to comfort me. His forebodings were too quickly realized ; for within a year of this time my pleasant childish life came to a sudden close, and I began the world.

CHAPTER II.

PASTORS AND MASTERS.

I HAD been gathering sticks in the woods with Margery one bright October afternoon, and came home loaded, with my little sister trotting merrily by my side, both of us happy in the consciousness of deserving mammy's praise for our labours. We came bounding into the cosy little kitchen; but finding no one there, threw down our burdens, and went in search of mammy. We paused, awe-struck, on the threshold of the parlour, that sacred Sabbath chamber, where portraits of King William and Queen Mary hung on each side of the chimney-piece, and where an earthenware pot of fresh flowers always adorned the somewhat cheerless hearth. In this room, so rarely used as to be in a manner a chamber of mystery, we beheld mammy seated in solemn converse with a stranger; a thin, pale-faced woman, dressed in black, and of a severe aspect; a woman whose face had been ploughed and ravaged by that dire scourge of those days, the small-pox, and at sight of whom little Margery uttered a faint shriek of terror, and immediately turned and fled. Not so myself, who stood transfixed by the strange vision.

'Is that the boy?' demanded the stranger sternly.

My foster-mother faltered an affirmative.

'Come hither, boy,' said the stranger; and I obeyed with fear and trembling.

Upon this she began to question me.

'What is your name?' she asked.

'Robin,' I mumbled.

'Robin what? Nothing but Robin, poor cast-away!'

She shook her head in a dismal manner, and groaned aloud. I think it was the first groan I had ever heard, and the sound appalled me.

'Robin is but a vulgar name for Robert,' she said. 'Can you read, Robert?'

I stared on hearing myself addressed by this new name.

'Is the boy an idiot?' cried the grim stranger.

'My name is Robin,' I answered; 'and I know nowt o' reading.'

This was true. In the circle in which I had lived,

reading and writing were unknown accomplish-ments.

The stranger shook her head again, more dismally than before.

'It is time you were taken in hand, Master Robert,' she said; and I hated her forthwith for this persistent alteration of my name. 'Would you like to live in a big house, and learn to read and write?'

'I'd rather stay with daddy and mammy,' I answered, sidling up to my foster-mother, who received me with a silent hug.

'And grow up a very heathen in the darkness of ignorance,' said the stranger. 'Happily for you, Master Robert, Providence does not permit us to choose our own paths, or few among us would be snatched from the burning. I have had a letter from my lady, bidding me take you to live at the great house, where my good husband will undertake your education.'

The whole of this speech might have been spoken in a foreign language for any comprehension I had of its meaning, except so far as it conveyed to me the one direful fact that I was to be separated from those I loved. I began to cry, and little Margery, who had crept back to the doorway, curious to observe the stranger, came running into the room, and flung her arms round my neck. Her affection conquered her terror of the grim stranger, and she looked defiance at the dame as she clung to me.

'Naughty 'ooman shan't take 'oo, Rob,' she cried; but her mother interposed, and laid a firm hand on the dear innocent's lips.

'We shall be very sorry to lose him, madam,' she said gently; 'he has been like our own child; and I wish my lady had given us longer notice before she took him away.'

'Hoity toity!' cried the dame indignantly; 'my lady thought she had to do with sensible people. You could not suppose you were to keep this boy all his life. He has to learn how to get an honest livelihood, that he mayn't be a burden on Lady Barbara to the end of the chapter, as some folks I would rather not mention were a burden upon my lady's father. He comes of a bad stock, Mistress Hawker; and running wild in the forest won't mend him.'

On this the keeper's wife hugged me closer to her honest heart.

'There is not a better child in Berkshire,' cried the tender soul, with some warmth.

Margery, perceiving, as by instinct, that I had been maligned, clung about me the closer; and thus bound together by grief and affection, and encircled by the mother's fond arms, we defied the intruder.

'I don't come of a bad stock, and I ain't a burden upon any one; and I don't want to live at the big house with the nasty black water round it;. and I don't like you, because you're ugly; and I won't leave mammy and daddy.'

'I wish you joy of your nurse-child, Margery Hawker,' cried the stranger, getting up from her chair in a great passion, and stalking to the door. 'His manners and his learning do you credit; and I'm sure my lady will be vastly pleased with you when she hears the good effects of your care.'

My foster-mother pleaded pardon for my innocence and ignorance, in a great fright, for Mrs. Grimshaw held a sceptre of regal sway at Hauteville Hall, during the prolonged absence of Sir Marcus and my lady. Margery and I were sent from the room in disgrace, and retired to weep together in the kitchen, where I plighted my youthful troth to the sweet young damsel, and swore that none but she should be my wife.

'I'll never go to the big ugly house, Sissy,' said I; 'but we'll be married, and live in the woods with the squirrels, and have nuts and berries for our dinner.'

'Yes; but some night we should die of hunger, and the robins would cover us with leaves; and mammy and daddy would be sorry,' cried Madge, who had heard the story of the Children in the Wood.

After this there came a few more careless days, during which Margery and I gathered wood in the forest, and hunted for nuts in the hazel-copses, and forgot that there was such a creature as black-robed Mrs. Grimshaw upon this world. Then came a bleak, bitter morning, when my foster-mother dressed me in my best clothes, and kissed and cried over me before she handed me to the executioner.

The executioner was a small sickly-looking man, dressed in a suit of chocolate-coloured cloth, and wearing a carefully-powdered wig. This gentleman I was told was Mr. Grimshaw, and to him, as to his stately spouse, I was to pay all possible respect.

'You'll let him come to see us sometimes, won't you, sir?' asked the keeper's wife piteously. 'He's been with us over nine years; and it's a sore trouble to lose him.'

' So it be, wife, a sore trouble,' growled the keeper.—' Thou'lt think on us sometimes, won't thee, Rob ? '

' Ay, ay, he shall think of you, and come to see you too,' replied the chocolate-coloured gentleman good-naturedly.

Even this little speech inclined me to prefer Mr. Grimshaw to his respectable consort.

' Thou'lt mind thy book, Robin, and do as thou art bid,' urged my foster-mother; ' and thy new friends will love thee; and thou'lt come to see thy old friends sometimes.'

' Every day, if they'll let me,' I answered, sobbing.

After this there were many embraces and many tears, until Mr. Grimshaw grew impatient, and said we must be gone. So I tore myself away from those dear souls, who had made my childhood happy, and put my hand into that of the house-steward.

The day was bleak and wintry, and we trudged off at a good rate among the crisp fallen leaves. I looked back at the keeper's cottage. Ah, dear home, mine no longer ! How many years were to pass before I should inhabit any other dwelling which I could dare call by the fond name of home! Mansion and palace, tent and dungeon, were to be my habitation in the shifting scenes of life; but long and far were to be my wanderings before I rested again beside so cheery a hearth, or among friends so dear.

The walk from the keeper's cottage to the Hall was a long one, and I had ample leisure in which to observe the countenance of my new guardian as I tramped by his side among the drift of withered leaves and the fallen fir-cones which I had gathered so merrily but yesterday with little Margery. It was not a hard or sour face at which I looked; and with the quick instinct of childhood I divined that this gentleman in the chocolate-coloured coat would be my friend. I pushed my hand a little farther into his, and drew closer to him as we walked on. For a long time we walked in silence, but by-and-by the old gentleman looked down at me with a curious glance.

'You are but a little chap to begin your schooling,' he said; 'but I see you are no fool, and I think you and I may get on well enough together.'

After this he questioned me for some time about

my past life and its simple pleasures, and conversed with me kindly until we came to our destination. We did not pass beneath the shadow of the great gothic archway; that ponderous gateway had not been opened since Lady Barbara Lestrange's last residence at Hauteville. We crossed a narrow stone bridge of modern construction, which spanned the moat upon the inferior side of the Hall, and entered the house by a little door, the key whereof my companion took from his capacious pocket.

Within, I saw shadowy stone passages that seemed endless, innumerable doors of darkest oak. The silence and gloom of the place were awful to my childish mind. I clung closer to Mr. Grimshaw, and shuddered at the echoing noise of our footsteps on the smooth stone flags. We crossed a great hall where tattered rags of many-coloured silks hung from the vaulted roof, and where shone upon me, for the first time in my life, the splendour of an old stained-glass window.

The floor of this chamber was of alternate squares of black and white marble. The effigy of a mailed knight, bestriding a plumed war-steed of painted wood, shone in the rainbow light from the great window; and at the opposite end of the hall a staircase, with elaborately-carved balustrades in black oak, led to a gallery which made the circuit of the roof.

At this chamber I gazed with delight and wonder, and for the moment forgot my awe of the gloomy house. From the hall my companion led me into a long saloon, with ten windows, overlooking a small Italian flower-garden, within the moat : and from this we passed to another long room, where I beheld more books than I could have supposed were contained in all the world, seeing that one volume— a clumsy leather-bound ' breeches ' Bible—com- prised the keeper's entire library. From wall to ceiling this long and lofty room was lined with volumes, for the most part in handsome, though somewhat sombre, bindings. Wings had been con- structed, abutting into the room, for the accommoda- tion of more books ; and these abutments divided the spacious apartment into pleasant nooks and retiring-places, where I thought it must needs be very agreeable to sit on a bright summer day, when the flowers in the pleasaunce were all in bloom.

' See, Master Robert,' said my new friend.   ' You open your eyes wide at the sight of so many books.

What would you say if I told you that I had read them every one, or, at any rate, know the contents of every one—from the big brown folios down yonder to the smart little duodecimos on those narrow shelves near the ceiling? I was my late lord's librarian as well as his house-steward, and all these books are still in my care, and are likely to be till I die: and then I know not how it will fare with them, for books are like children, and must be cared for by those that love them.'

He hurried me from the library—where I would fain have stood gaping longer—by a small door almost hidden between two book-cases. This door led us away from the light and sunshine into a dark and narrow passage, at the end of which Mr. Grimshaw opened another door, and pushed me into a square oak-panelled room, where I beheld the black-robed woman whom I had seen at the keeper's cottage.

She was sitting at a table working, with a great wicker-basket before her. She laid down her work as we entered, and gazed upon me with menacing eyes.

My heart sank as I encountered those searching glances.

c 2

' So, Master Robert, you have come at last. I began to think that you and my husband were lost in the woods.'

I almost wished that this misfortune had befallen us, as I quailed beneath Mrs. Grimshaw's stern gaze. Surely the berries and the robins and the brief summer-day life of children abandoned in the forest would have been better than existence shared with Mrs. Grimshaw.

' Now, Master Robert,' said that lady, ' this is where you are to live until you go out into the world to earn your own bread, which will be as soon as you are old enough to turn your hand to an honest trade, or sit upon a junior-clerk's stool in a merchant's office. You are to live with me and my husband, and to learn what he teaches you, and to do as I bid you, or it will be the worse for you. And mark you, young gentleman, there is to be no gadding about the park, or sneaking down to John Hawker's cottage, to waste your time among vagabonds and idlers.'

She spoke to me as if I had been fifteen years old instead of ten. But there was one part of her speech I understood well enough.

' My daddy is no vagabond,' I cried indignantly;

' and this gentleman said I should go and see him.'

' Ay, ay, I promised as much as that,' answered Mr. Grimshaw with an apologetic air. ' Hawker and his wife seemed so sorry to lose the boy, and the boy cried at leaving them; and I could not well avoid promising——'

' You're a fool, Anthony Grimshaw,' cried his wife angrily.

She rang a bell, which was promptly answered by a plump rosy-faced woman in a mob-cap and big white apron.

' This is the young gentleman, Betty,' said Mrs. Grimshaw; ' take him to his room, and see that he washes his face and hands before he comes back to dinner.'

The maid led me off through the dark passage and up a narrow wooden staircase, into a small whitewashed chamber, neatly but poorly furnished. This room she told me was mine; and as it was superior to any chamber in Jack Hawker's cottage, I felt somewhat proud of the proprietorship.

' Has Mrs. Grim been unkind to you, boy?' asked Betty, as she scrubbed my face, exhibiting a merciless prodigality in the matter of soap.

'Mrs. Grim?'

'Pshaw! Grimshaw, child. We call her Mrs. Grim for short. The name fits her to a T; but Mrs. Brimstone would be still better; for brimstone she is, and brimstone she ever will be. Has she been scolding you?'

'She has not been very kind,' I answered, whimpering.

'No, and it ain't in her nature; so don't expect it. She was turned sour close upon twelve years ago, when a fine gentleman that she'd have given her eyes for laughed and talked and made a fool of her with his pretty speeches and pretty looks, and then walked off and forgot all about her. *I know!* She took the small-pox after that, and lost her beauty, which was never much to my mind, and *that* didn't mend her temper. She hasn't had a civil word for anybody since then; and how old Grim could have been such a fool as to marry her, unless she frightened him into it, I can't think. But he did; and now she's turned methody, and is always going after preachings at the places round about, and leads us all the life of dogs.'

Thus did Mrs. Betty give vent to her opinions while engaged with my toilet; and it is to be observed

that from this time forth I became the habitual
recipient of confidences ill adapted to my tender
years. People who have but few companions with
whom to converse will find relief in opening their
minds to a little child; and whether it was Anthony
Grimshaw who dilated on the history of the house
he served, or Mrs. Betty who reviled her mistress, I
listened with equal patience, and with no small interest; and being henceforth cut off for the most part
from intercourse with children, and denied all childish
sports, I acquired a gravity and a curious spirit not
common to my age.

When Betty had scrubbed and brushed me into a
becoming state of redness and stiffness, she conducted me back to the oak parlour, where I dined in
state with my new guardians, attended on by Betty in
a clean white apron.

Mrs. Grimshaw found a great deal to say about
my boorish demeanour, and the ill-use I made of
knife and fork, the former of which I was indeed
accustomed to use with a freedom and a dexterity
unknown in polished circles. The dinner was of
the plainest, but served with much neatness; and
after the cloth had been removed Mrs. Grimshaw
kept the obsequious Betty employed for a quarter of

an hour in polishing the walnut-wood table on which we had dined.

Even after this operation Betty was not free to depart, for Mrs. Grimshaw bade her seat herself at a respectful distance, in order to hear the conclusion of a sermon, one-half of which she had been edified by upon the previous day.

'And I hope you feel some inward benefit from Mr. Whitefield's precious eloquence, Betty,' said Mrs. Grimshaw. 'I grieve to say there are some rocky hearts upon which the blessed seed falls in vain; some heathenish minds that prefer to pore over any dusty rubbish in a foreign language, rather than to hear the voice of the mighty Judge calling sinners to judgment.'

Her looks were directed at her husband during the latter part of this speech, and he, by his answer, acknowledged that it was levelled at him.

'Why, truth to tell, Martha,' he said, 'there may be some that are not inclined to stand before Mr. Whitefield for judgment. If I am to be brought to believe that one section of mankind is destined for grace, and the rest doomed to perdition unspeakable, and that our good works and gentle deeds in this world shall avail us nothing with Him who promised

His blessing in exchange for a cup of cold water
given to His disciple, I will be taught by Calvin at
first hand, and not Mr. Whitefield at second hand.
We have the Genevese edition of John Calvin's
works, in twelve folio volumes, in the library yonder;
and I can read the " Institutes " for myself if needs
be. But it has been my custom to smoke my pipe
on the terrace after dinner for the last five-and-thirty
years of my life; and with your leave, wife, I shall
continue to do so, till pipe and I go out together.'
By this I perceived that old Anthony Grimshaw was
not completely under his wife's dominion.

'Will you come with me, Master Bob?' he
asked; and I sprang up, eager to follow him.

Mrs. Grimshaw groaned aloud.

'The boy will stop, for the profit of his sinful
soul,' she said, in a tone of command. 'Sit down
over against Betty, child.'

I seated myself meekly, while Mr. Grimshaw
lighted his pipe, and went out by a half-glass door
that opened on the terrace—a noble promenade going
all round the house, and bordered on this side by a
bank close planted with evergreens sloping to the
broad moat.

Then began the reading of Mr. Whitefield's

sermon, which was performed in a hard, harsh voice
by Mrs. Grimshaw. Of the sermon I know no more
than that it was of appalling and threatening import,
and that it seemed to my childish ears interminable.
Betty yawned more than once; and on one occasion
I saw her on the point of sinking into a peaceful
slumber; but she caught herself up with an effort,
and stared at her mistress with unblinking eyes
when that lady turned her gaze towards the hand-
maiden. When that discourse was at last ended,
Betty declared herself beyond measure edified, but
seemed, nevertheless somewhat glad to withdraw.

Mr. Grimshaw had passed the window several
times during the pious lecture, and appeared at the
glass door, still smoking, a few minutes after it was
over.

'May I go to the gentleman, ma'am?' I asked;
and Mrs. Grimshaw having nodded assent, I ran out
and put my hand into that of her husband, who
received me with a kind smile.

' I like you so much,' I said, ' because you're kind,
like daddy, though you don't speak like him.'

From this time forth Anthony Grimshaw and I
were fast friends; and the old man's gentle treatment enabled me to endure his wife's harsh usage

with all due meekness. Her conduct never varied.
Stern and sour in her bearing towards all her little
world, her manner to me betrayed an aversion which
she would fain have concealed. Hard, bitter, and
implacable as my own evil fate, she cast her venge-
ful shadow across my boyhood; and if she could
have prevented the sun from shining on me, or could
have stunted my growth and wasted my flesh by the
influence of her baleful gaze, I believe she would
have exercised her evil power. It was not till later
that I obtained the key to the mystery of her feelings
with regard to me. She had, happily, little opportunity of doing me harm, for I was entrusted
to her keeping by a mistress whom she feared, and
whom self-interest compelled her to serve with submission and fidelity. She could, however, make my
life more or less uncomfortable by small cruelties
and petty slights, by cold looks and bitter words;
and this privilege she exercised without stint. Had
it not been for her husband's kindness I might have
fared ill in that splendid mansion, where I was a
humble and nameless dependent; but his goodness
to me never wavered, nor did his protection ever fail
me in the hour of need.

My first night in my lonely chamber was a very

sad one. In my dreams I went back to the warrener's lodge and the dear souls I loved; but even in those dreams the bitter sense of separation clung to me, and I felt that I saw the familiar faces across an impassable gulf.

My studies began on the next day, in the parlour where Mrs. Grimshaw sat at work; and I felt her eyes upon me while I was being initiated into the mysteries of the alphabet by my friend Anthony. From this time my life became an unvarying routine. Early breakfast in the oak parlour, a walk with Mr. Grimshaw about the house or in the wide-flagged quadrangle, where a Hercules and his club held guard over a vast marble basin which had once been the glory of the place. Then back to the oak parlour for lessons, which lasted till the early dinner. Then Mrs. Grimshaw's lecture from the last-published pamphlets of Whitefield or Wesley, or some minor lights of the new nonconforming church, and Betty's smothered yawns, and Anthony Grimshaw's figure passing to and fro before the windows, and my own weariness always in precisely the same measure. At six we drank tea; a solemn ceremony, in the gentility whereof Mrs. Grimshaw took much pride. At half-past eight she read prayers to her husband

and myself, and to the three servants of the great melancholy house,—Betty, a buxom girl called Martha, and a rheumatic old woman, who lived in some stony obscurity in the kitchens, and rarely quitted her lair except for this evening ceremonial.

After prayers I was hustled off to my chamber by Betty, while my guardians supped together in grim state. I should often have gone to bed hungry if it had not been for Betty, who brought me a hunch of bread and a basin of milk, which I ate and drank seated on the edge of my bed with more enjoyment than I ever derived from the ceremonial meals in the oak parlour. On Sundays there were no lessons, but there was chapel—to my youthful mind a far greater trial. Mr. Grimshaw went on alternate Sundays to the little church in the wood, and to have gone thither with him would have been happiness unspeakable to me, for at this time-honoured tabernacle I should have met Jack Hawker and his wife, and dear little Margery. But here Mrs. Grimshaw had a convenient opportunity for exercising her tyranny, and avenging that unconscious sin which I had committed against her by coming into this bleak world. So she ordained that I should accompany herself and the two maids to the meeting-house at Warborough,—a stifling upper room, little better than a loft, in which the Rev. Simeon Noggers, an awakened tailor, held forth every Sunday to a select congregation of Wesleyans. In this airless chamber I underwent the tortures of a weekly suffocation while the Rev. Simeon pounded his deal reading-desk and exhorted his fellow-sinners, from the blackness of whose guilt he appeared to derive a dismal satisfaction. From that respectable teacher I learned that it was rather advantageous for the soul to be dyed of the darkest hue, in order that its renovation might be the more astounding. There I heard no exhortations to the weak and wavering; no friendly counsel for the small debtor, whose payments were but a little in arrear, and who needed only a steadfast endeavour to set his affairs in order and regain a solvent condition. The Reverend Simeon addressed his flock as if convinced that they were so many fraudulent bankrupts, conscious that they could never pay a shilling in the pound, and rather to be congratulated than otherwise on their ignominious insolvency.

'Believe!' cried the awakened Noggers, 'and prove your faith as I do, not as St. Paul did. Prove it by long prayers and reiterated invocations, in which the

reverent address of the Christian to his Lord is super-
seded by a blasphemous familiarity ; prove it by
howlings and beatings of the breast, by upturned eyeballs, and solemn shakings of the head, and arrogant
condemnation of all mankind except the elect of
Warborough.'

This was the gist of Mr. Nogger's teaching, which
I heard during the ten most impressionable years of
my life, and which did much to make me in early
manhood a disciple of Bolingbroke and Hobbes. It
fell to my lot in after years to hear both Wesley and
Whitefield, and I then perceived the difference between a man of original mind and deep-rooted con-
victions, and the ignorant imitators who assume his
functions without one of the gifts that have qualified
their master for his office. I know that to that good
man John Wesley there came much trouble and per-
plexity from the ill-advised officiousness and spasmodic
industry of some among his followers. Doubtless he
found other labourers better fitted to work with him
in the vineyard ; and it must never be forgotten that
the uprising of the sect which bears his name has
done much to arouse the slr g ;ards of the Established
Church, who had sore need of some revolution to
awaken them from their guilty slumber.

For nearly ten years my life at Hauteville was all of the same pattern; my studies laborious, my pleasures of the rarest.   Indeed, the only holiday I knew in these days was an occasional visit to Jack Hawker's cottage, and Mrs. Grimshaw took care that I should not often enjoy this happiness. The distance was long, and my task-mistress contrived to find reasons for refusing me the leisure required for such a visit. It was only when Anthony Grimshaw interfered in my behalf that I was allowed the privilege of an afternoon's holiday. Dearly, then, did I love the long walk through the park, the cosy supper by Jack Hawker's hearth, and the return in the dewy moonlight to the great enchanted castle, which, even after years of residence, still retained for me something of its awful charm.

Although to the last degree monotonous, my life during these years was not unhappy. In Anthony Grimshaw I had a true friend, and such a tutor as few prosperous young noblemen of my day could have boasted.   From the hour in which he first introduced me to the hieroglyphics of the English alphabet to the proud day in which he smiled upon my successful rendering of a love-ditty by Rochester in to Anacreontics in pure Greek, he made the steeps of

Parnassus easy, and the waters of Pieria sweet for
me. It was a delight to him to have some one to
whom to impart his ripe store of history and legend,
and he found me a willing and enraptured listener
to that cherished lore. I knew every biography in
Plutarch, and every adventure of Ulysses, before I
could read the easiest page in my spelling-book; and
I was lured on through the slough of despond which
the juvenile student must pass, by the knowledge that
the great brown-backed folios in the library contained
innumerable stories delightful as those my master
told me. The time came when very few of the
brown-backed volumes contained any mystery for
me, and when I could read alike easily in English,
French, Italian, and Latin; and from that time
forth my chief pleasure was found in the long library,
where I used to spend my leisure hours curled up in
one of the deep-recessed windows, with a folio on my
knees.

The noble Elizabethan mansion was a source of
perpetual pleasure to me. The great empty rooms
reverberated with the echo of my footsteps as I roamed
at large, with my tutor's official bunch of keys in my
pocket. The very poetry of ghostliness pervaded
those spacious untenanted chambers. All was swept

and garnished; there was no trace of dust, no token
of neglect; but the emptiness was none the less
dismal. The house had the unmistakable air of a
long-deserted habitation. All the brightness had
faded from curtains and carpets, the gilding was tarnished, the paint was worn and dull; the stillness of
rooms that had once been noisy with the bustle and
grandeur of state-reception and familiar assembly was
more oppressive than the solemn calm of a churchyard. But to me there was a subtle delight in that
dead calm, that utter stillness. My imagination ran
riot in those empty chambers. At will I peopled
them with the shade of the mighty dead. The Virgin
Queen revisited the house where she had been gor-
geously entertained by the first Baron Hauteville;
and I saw her in all her great littleness, the cynosure
of statesmen and flatterers, philosophers and syco-
phants, lovers who never loved her, courtiers who
dared not trust her, ambassadors who registered her
every look and word for swift transmission to their
masters, spies who watched in the Stuart interest,
and hungered for the hour when this great queen
should be dust. Swift passed that radiant vision of
queenly grandeur and human weakness, and lo! the
rush and terror of civil war. Buffets ransacked of

their gold and silver store; plate melted, or sold to foreign Jews; trusty captains playing at hide-and-seek in chimneys and secret closets; Cromwell's grim soldiers battering at the gates. A sudden cry of horror through the land; halls hung with black; bells tolling slow and solemn in the wintry morning, and England kingless.

Again the scene changes, and it is the garish summer noontide of the Restoration.

'Room there for my Lord Rochester!' cried the lackeys by the great gilded doors of the white and gold banquet-hall; 'way there, knaves, for his grace the Duke of Buckingham!' and athwart the slanting shaft of motes dancing in the sunshine came the shadows of Wilmot and Villiers, in their silken embroidered suits of French make, with long curling perukes and ribbon-befringed jerkins, stars and orders blazing on their breasts, and a languid light in their eyes. As I sat by the cold empty hearth, and mused, with dreamy gaze fixed on the opposite doorway, the room grew crowded with the notabilities of the Restoration; I could almost hear the fluttering fringes and sword-knots of those butterfly lordlings; but with a thought they vanished; and here was hook-nosed William, grave and silent as

his mighty ancestor; and courteous St. John, and
brilliant Harley, and anon all the wits and beaux,
generals and statesmen, who embellished the reign
of dull Queen Anne.

Not alone with the great whom I had read of did
I people those desolate rooms. At my bidding
other shadows grew into life. From the canvas on
the walls of picture-gallery and saloon, the images
of the dead descended to walk again in the rooms
they had inhabited living.   Hautevilles of the
Elizabethan age, and Hautevilles of the Restoration;
Hautevilles who fought in the Low Countries with
Marlborough, and sat in the senate with Harley:
about these, of whose histories I then knew so little,
I dreamed my dreams. This dark cavalier had
loved and won that fair-haired maiden with tender
blue eyes and simple pastoral dress; that smooth-
faced boy-soldier had wooed and been scorned by
the haughty damsel with eagle glance and towering
headgear.

For each of these pictured faces I wove my little
romance, but was not the less eager to extort some
details of their actual lives from my kindly tutor.

I often plied him with questions about the dead-
and-gone masters of that deserted house; but with

varying success. He was no gossip or scandal-monger; and, indeed, was so complete a student, that he thought more of a rare edition of an original classic, or a translation of the sixteenth century, than of all the changes and chances of the age in which he lived. An occasional *Postboy* kept him apprised of the conquests our arms achieved abroad, and the difficulty our ministers found in agreeing at home. But he thought more of the Philippics of Cicero than of a smart attack from the opposition, or a scathing reply from the polished chief of the famous Broad-bottom Administration; and was far better acquainted with the politics of the Pompeian party than with the objects and opinions of the minority at Westminster. Sometimes I was happy enough to find him in a communicative mood; and then I took care to improve my opportunity.

CHAPTER III.

I AM CURIOUS ABOUT THE PAST.

THE time came when anxiety to know the story of my own birth grew keener than my interest in the day-dreams with which I was wont to beguile my hours of solitude. It was on this subject that I questioned Anthony Grimshaw as we sat together in the library one bleak March evening, when the wind blew hoarsely in the great oaks and beeches across the moat, and the wood-fire burning on the low hearth made a cheery glow in the spacious room, gleaming now on the russet and crimson bindings of the books, now on the stout beams and carved oak bosses of the ceiling.

I was nineteen years of age, and older and graver than my years by reason of the monotony of my life and the gravity of my companions. It was not the first time I had questioned Anthony Grimshaw upon the subject of my own history.

' I think you know more than you choose to tell,'
I said.

'Nay, Robert, I know nothing. I may have my
suspicions. But what good would it do for me to
talk of such fancies? It might be but to mislead
you. All I *know* is that Lady Barbara brought you
here one winter's night in the first year of her
marriage. She travelled in a postchaise with her
maid—a Frenchwoman, whom she engaged on her
marriage, my wife speaking no language but her own,
and being therefore unadapted for residence abroad
with an ambassador's lady,—leaving Sir Marcus in
London, where he was busy with public matters, she
said. You were a baby of less than a year old, and as
sickly an infant as ever survived infancy. She sent
for Martha, who had been married to me but a few
months, and told her that she meant to adopt the
child, having Sir Marcus's permission for so doing;
which well she might, seeing that she was an heiress
and a beauty, and might have married much higher
if she had so chosen.'

' And she gave your wife no account of my birth?'
I asked.

'None that I ever heard. But Martha Grimshaw
can keep a secret. I know she has her suspicions,

which jump with mine; and that's why she has not been as kind to you as I should have wished. There was a gentleman once lived in this house whose fate it was to carry mischief and misfortune with him wherever he went.'

' Who was that gentleman ? '

' Roderick Ainsleigh, the only son of my late lord's only sister, Lady Susan Somerton, and Colonel Ainsleigh, a brave soldier and a dissipated spendthrift, whom she married against the earl's wish, and with whom her life was most miserable. She died young, while the colonel was abroad with his regiment, leaving an only child but just nine years old. This was the boy Roderick. Lord Hauteville brought him here directly after the mother's death; and the next post from the Low Countries brought home news that the colonel had been killed at the head of his regiment. He had ever been as reckless of his life as of his fortune, and had been oftener under fire than any other man of his age and standing. Thus you see the boy was doubly an orphan.'

' Poor child ! '

' 'Tis natural you should pity him, lad; but that double bereavement was the most fortunate event in Roderick Ainsleigh's life. The earl, my late master,

one of the noblest and best of men, had loved his
only sister with extreme tenderness and devotion.
Her death and the death of her husband threw the
boy entirely into his uncle's hands. My lord loved
the child at once for the mother's sake ; and the
boy's handsome face and winning manners did the
rest. Those soft pleasing manners disguised as
proud a heart as ever beat in human breast; but I
think my lord loved the boy all the more for his daring
spirit. It was only in after years that he found how
hard it is to govern a stubborn will, even when self-
interest is at stake.'

' Was the boy happy here ?'

' He had reason to be ; for if he had been the
earl's son and heir he could not have fared better, or
been treated with greater honour by all who lived in
the house and all who came to it. I was his first
schoolmaster, and taught him just as I have taught
you. Often when you and I have been sitting side
by side in yonder window—'twas on that very spot
Roderick and I used to sit—I have fancied I was
twenty years younger, and that 'twas Roderick Ainsleigh I was teaching. But he was neither so diligent
nor so obedient a pupil as you, Robert. His mind
iwas quck enough, and he would work hard enough

sometimes, in his own impetuous way. But it was all by fits and starts—blow hot, blow cold. I had another pupil who very often shared Mr. Roderick's lessons, and that was Lady Barbara Somerton, my lord's only child; and it was not long before I discovered that the two young people loved each other with an affection that was something more than mere cousinship. Lord Hauteville liked to see them together, and was pleased to find his daughter desired to be wiser than most young women of her age. " I would have thee as clever as Lady Mary Wortley, or Mde. de Sevigné, Bab," he used to say. One day he broached the subject of the liking between his daughter and his nephew, and told me that nothing would please him better than to see his sister Susan's son master of Hauteville. "I don't care to think of a stranger cutting down the old beeches, or clearing the plantations that you and I planned when we were boys together, Tony," he said. "And, tie up the estate as I may upon my daughter, I can't tie up every old tree and every footpath in the wood. And I like to think the place will be the same for years to come, when my old bones are mouldering in the vault yonder, which it might if one of my own flesh and blood were master. A stranger has no feeling for old timber. Roderick ought to love every tree, for he has almost grown up in the park and woods."'

'And was Mr. Roderick Ainsleigh very fond of his cousin?' I asked.

'He seemed to love her as dearly as she loved him; and I don't suppose it was all seeming. He went to Cambridge when he was nineteen, and I was proud to think that he was a better mathematician than most men of thirty, and would do wonders; but he got into a bad set at the University, and gave himself up to the wild pleasures of that place, which is within a ride of Newmarket, that infamous seminary of iniquity and ill-manners. Nothing but trouble ensued from Mr. Ainsleigh's residence at Cambridge. He incurred debts which would have been heavy had he been Lord Hauteville's sole heir; and my lord paid them, but not without protest, and some ill blood between the uncle and nephew. His visits here were few and brief, and it was evident to all of us that Lady Barbara resented the evil courses into which he had fallen. When he came he brought with him college-friends, wild young fellows, who attended all the fairs and races round about, lamed my lord's hacks and hunters, and turned the heads of half the servant-maids at Hauteville'

'He must have been a base ungrateful fellow,' I cried indignantly.

'Ungrateful he most assuredly was. Whether he was by nature base, or only reckless and extravagant under the influence of ill-advisers, I cannot tell. As a lad I loved him dearly, in spite of his wilfulness; but when I saw the unhappiness caused by his conduct as a young man, I was inclined to doubt whether he had ever been worthy of the affection we all lavished upon him. For four years things went on thus, with much trouble for the earl, of which he made no secret, and profound sorrow for Lady Barbara, who maintained a proud silence upon the subject of her grief, but whose despondency was too obvious to all who loved her,—except perhaps to the offender himself, whom she treated with a haughty distance which must have been to the last degree galling to that proud spirit. He for his part affected an indifference to her ill opinion, and even told me in confidence, that since his cousin had ceased to love him, he cared not a doit how badly she thought of him. I would fain have persuaded him that he was still beloved, but he laughed me to scorn. "Why, she is kinder to her lap-dog than to me," he cried; "and when I have essayed to obtain her pardon for my manifold iniquities, she has received my apologies with such black looks as speedily silenced me." One day the storm, long threatened, burst in sudden fury. There was a desperate quarrel between Lord Haute-ville and his nephew, in which my lord reproached Mr. Ainsleigh with his ingratitude, and reminded him of his dependence. Roderick Ainsleigh was the last of men to brook such humiliation. He boldly asserted his independence, and in proof thereof declared that he would never again owe a favour to the kins-man who had so degraded him. " I would rather take the king's shilling than eat the bread of dependence," he said ; " and I thank your lordship for reminding me that I have no right to the bounties I have enjoyed at your hands. I blame my own dulness for my having so long remained unconscious of my abject position, and am glad to be awakened to the truth, though the waking has been somewhat rough. For the past I must remain your debtor, and I confess the debt is a heavy one ; happily, the future is my own, and I can promise that it shall cost you but little."

' Upon this Mr. Ainsleigh flung himself out of the room with such an air of offended manhood, that my lord confessed he felt himself the aggressor.

" He will come back, Tony," he said to me, when his nephew had left Hauteville, which he did directly after the interview. " Sure, he knows I love him as a son, and am but too weakly disposed to excuse his errors, nor can I think that he has ceased to love my little Barbara, though the two do not seem such fast friends as they once were." '

' And did the young man come back?' I asked, deeply concerned.

' Never since that day has Roderick Ainsleigh crossed the threshold of this house. Whether he is living or dead none here can tell, though there is one who would, I doubt not, be glad to know the truth. He went straight from here to Cambridge, and it came to my lord's ears by-and-by that he had lost money to his Newmarket friends, over and above the debts my master had paid, and was in some sort a defaulter. If he had come back I know he would have been received with open arms; but my lord was too proud to invite his return. He had left but a year when his uncle died. The title died with him, and Lady Barbara, as sole heiress, became mistress of the estate. When her mourning was over she went to London to visit the Honourable Mr. and Mrs. Davenant, relations of her mother; and while

residing with them she married Sir Marcus Lestrange,
a widower of high family and small fortune, but of
much political influence.   She spent a few months
here with her husband soon after their marriage, and
then departed, to return no more except for that
flying visit when you were brought hither.'

'But was nothing more ever heard of Mr.
Ainsleigh ?'

'No further tidings of that misguided young man
ever reached my ears, except one painful rumour,
which connected the flight of a clergyman's daughter
from her father's house near this place with the
name of Roderick Ainsleigh. How justly I know
not. Slander fattens upon the misdoings of the
absent. The young man was not here to defend
himself against these evil reports, and I doubt not
they had some influence with his cousin, Lady
Barbara.'

'What was he like?' I asked ; 'I have seen no
picture of him in the house.'

'Ay, but his portrait was painted. It used to
hang above this chimney-piece, but it was taken
down and thrust away at my lord's desire when his
nephew had been some six months absent without
any sign of repentance. "Take that ungrateful

boy's face from my sight," he said, "it haunts me like a bad dream." Would you like to see Roderick Ainsleigh's likeness ? '

' Yes, that I should, mightily.'

The old man crossed the room and opened a cupboard in the wainscot beneath one of the windows.

' Light a candle, Robert,' he called to me as he groped on his knees before the open cupboard.

I took a candle from the chimney-piece, and lighted it by the blaze of the wood-fire.

' Bring your light here,' he cried ; and I went to him, and held the flickering candle before a frameless picture which he held upright upon a table near the window.

' 'Tis a good twenty years since that has seen the light,' he said, wiping the dust from the mildew-stained canvas.

It was the portrait of a man in the dawn of youth, a dark handsome face with a bright smile, but a look of indomitable pride in the eyes, which were black as a Spaniard's.

' Have you ever seen such a face as that, Robert ?' asked my tutor.

' I can scarce tell,' I answered thoughtfully ; ' but the features seem familiar to me.'

'Seem familiar; ay, lad, and so they must. Think again, Bob. Where have you seen that face?'

'In the glass!' I cried, with a great start. 'O, for God's sake, Anthony Grimshaw, tell me the truth, if you can!—was Roderick Ainsleigh my father?'

'In good sooth, Robert, I cannot tell. I have told you all that I know. But you and my late master's nephew are like as—I'll not say two drops of water, for there is little waterishness in your dispositions— you are as like as two flames of fire.'

CHAPTER IV.

I AM INTRODUCED TO MY BENEFACTRESS.

I MIGHT have brooded long on Anthony Grimshaw's strange revelation but for the rapid succession of events which followed within a short time of the conversation I have recorded.

After an enchanted sleep of nearly twenty years the castle in Hauteville woods suddenly awoke to life, and the monotonous calm of our existence was exchanged for all the stir and clamour which accompanies the sound of many voices, the tread of many feet, and the bustling industry of a full household.

It was upon a lovely evening in June that the spell which had so long held Hauteville Hall was suddenly broken. Not a word, not a whisper of rumour's busy tongue, had prepared my guardians or myself for the startling transformation. Anthony Grimshaw's indifference to the political events of his own time had kept him ignorant of ministerial

changes at home, and of our diplomatic relations
abroad, or he might have apprehended the possibility
of Sir Marcus Lestrange's recall from Madrid, where
he had been our plenipotentiary for some years.

Mr. Grimshaw and I were walking on the terrace
in the pleasant summer sunset, while my tutor's
stern partner was occupied with her incessant needle-
work by one of the windows of the oak parlour. Her
sharp gray eyes watched us as we paced to and fro,
and I doubt not it vexed her to see us in such
friendly communion, as it most assuredly vexed her
to find me impervious to the slights she put upon
me, and indifferent to her ill-will. Again on this
evening we talked of Roderick Ainsleigh, of whom
I had indeed often spoken since I had seen the
portrait hidden in the library-closet.

'Surely there can be little doubt of his death,' I
said, ' or some tidings of him must have reached you
in all these years.'

'It would seem likely, unless he has gone to push
his fortunes abroad, as he may have done, under a
feigned name, perhaps. He was ever a rank Jacobite,
and got himself into no little trouble here and at
Cambridge on that score. It was his nature, or his
humour, to oppose those who loved him ; and as the

earl was a stanch Hanoverian, my young gentleman must needs toss off his wine to the king over the water. If he was living in forty-five, I would wager he was amongst the rebel crew that disturbed peaceful Englishmen in that year. He loved fighting and riot and intrigue, and would have refused to serve the best of rightful sovereigns if there was but a wrongful one to plot and fight for. I doubt there are always a number of these rebellious spirits, these innate revolutionaries, to create and foster rebellion. Few men ever have life's highway made so smooth and easy for them as it was made for Roderick Ainsleigh; but you see, he preferred to scramble through brake and brier, and lose himself in a forest of guilt and sorrow.'

'You speak of him bitterly.'

'I cannot well refrain from bitterness, though I loved the lad well, and took rare pride in his teaching. But he broke my old master's heart, and went near to break Lady Barbara's; for I doubt if all her fashion and grandeur at foreign courts have ever made her as happy as she was in the old days, when she and her cousin Roderick used to study the classics together, and stroll in the garden yonder on summer evenings.'

'She must have been very beautiful in those days,' I said, 'if she was like her portrait in the picture-gallery.'

'The portrait barely does justice to her features and complexion. But there was a sparkling brightness in her countenance which no painter could ever seize. It was such a changing face. A landscape in oils will give you the face of the country-side and the steady sunshine of a midsummer noon, but not the play and flicker of the light that comes and goes upon the meadows twenty times in a minute. She told her sorrow to no one when her cousin left Hauteville, but the changeful brightness of her beauty faded from that hour.'

'Was the marriage with Sir Marcus Lestrange a love-match?'

'I doubt it. The Somertons are not given to change; and I do not think Lady Barbara could so soon have forgotten her cousin. But she was alone in the world, and an heiress, and doubtless felt her unprotected position.'

We talked some time longer of the house which my tutor had served so faithfully, and in the service whereof he hoped to end his days. The sun sloped westward behind a bank of foliage that looked black

against that golden light. Patches of crimson lit
up the westward side of the great brown trunks of
rugged elm and oak, and flashed still brighter on
the smooth silvery bark of the beeches. Belated
crows sailed across the tender upper gray, making
for their nests in the oldest elms. Thrush and
blackbird sang their vesper-hymn; and pensive from
some mysterious thicket sounded the song of the
nightingale. The distant water-pools reddened in
the reddening sunlight, and the stillness and calm
glory that belong to this one hour alone possessed
our souls, as we stopped in silence to lean lazily
upon the marble balustrade of the terrace and watch
the sinking sun.

While we thus watched, a sound so unfrequent
as to be startling roused each from his reverie.

It was the sound of carriage-wheels—the wheels
of not one only, but several vehicles. Anthony
Grimshaw and I regarded each other in silent
amazement, and then the old man hurried to the end
of the terrace, whence he could obtain a view of the
broad gravelled drive leading to the great gates.

I followed closely on his heels, to the full as eager
as himself.

Three carriages were winding slowly up the hill;

the foremost a handsome travelling-chariot with four
horses and smartly-dressed postboys ; the two others
clumsier vehicles, each drawn by two horses.

'It must be Sir Marcus, or my lady!' cried
Anthony ; 'who else should come here with such a
train? Run, boy! bid Martha have the doors
opened, and the shutters in the library and saloon,
and a fire lighted in the great hall, for it strikes
deadly cold in summer-time. And tell Betty and
Sue to stir themselves. The carriages will be at the
gate in less than five minutes.'

'I'll open the shutters with my own hands!' I
cried, and ran off to the oak parlour, where I dashed
open the half-glass door, and burst into the room,
to the horror of Martha Grimshaw.

'What now, you unmannerly jackanapes?' she
asked. I told her who was at hand. She started
from her chair and stood before me, deadly pale and
trembling ; never had I seen her so affected.

'My lady!' she exclaimed. 'It can't be.'

'But it is, Mrs. Grimshaw. Who else should it
be? There'll be wax-candles wanted for the saloon ;
'twill be dark in half-an-hour. Shall I run and bid
them open the doors?'

'Yes, yes,' she answered in a strange, absent way ;

and I left her still standing rooted to the ground, with a scared, pale face.

By this I perceived that there was one person in the world of whom the steward's wife stood in awe.

The bell in the gothic archway sounded with a great clanging stroke as I ran to call the maids. Betty went flying to the gate, and Anthony Grimshaw appeared at the same moment with a ponderous bunch of keys, ready to perform his office of seneschal. Susan, the second maid, went with me to open the shutters of the great saloon. We lighted the wax-candles scattered here and there in crystal candelabra, and the feeble lights twinkled faintly in the dusky chamber. I went on to the library to open the shutters there, while Susan stayed behind to kindle the logs on the wide stone hearth. I heard the sound of several voices, and the echoing patter of high heels on the marble floor of the hall; and then from the half-open door of the library I saw Mr. Grimshaw usher the unexpected visitors into the saloon.

Two ladies and a gentleman followed him into the dimly-lighted room. The ladies were so hooded and muffled that I saw but little of their faces. One was of a commanding figure, the other slender and graceful as the tall white lilies in the Italian garden. The elder lady sank into an arm-chair, with a sigh of fatigue, and flung off her black-silk hood and cloak. Yes, this was my Lady Barbara, as beautiful as the portrait with which I was so familiar, but of a more developed and regal beauty. Her dress was of a dark crimson brocade, her shoulders and arms veiled in a cloud of black lace. She wore powder, which became her admirably, and her full round throat, of marble whiteness, was encircled by a broad band of black velvet, clasped with a gem that seemed to emit a brighter flame than any of the tapers twinkling against the mirrors on the walls. Never, except in pictures, had I seen a woman of rank, and for the moment the vision somewhat dazzled my unaccustomed eyes.

The younger lady also removed her hood, and I beheld a pale, fair face, framed by loose unpowdered auburn hair. Such pale and fragile loveliness showed poorly beside the blaze of Lady Barbara's beauty; but I felt rather than saw that this young lady was beautiful.

The gentleman yawned aloud, and leaned with a listless air against the carved-oak chimney, amusing himself by kicking the smouldering logs with the toe of his boot.

'Damp wood, and a room that feels like a vault;
and, I conclude, very small probability of supper.
You should really have written to apprise your people
of your coming, Lady Barbara.'

The speaker was a young man, tall, slim, good-
looking, and dressed in a suit of cut velvet, with point-
lace ruffles and cravat. He wore high riding-boots,
and a court-sword dangled at his side. My only
acquaintance with this species was derived from Pope's
Rape of the Lock, and this gentleman reminded me
of Sir Plume.

'It was my humour to come unannounced,' replied
my lady somewhat haughtily; and then she addressed
her steward, in a much sweeter tone. 'You will not
let us go to bed supperless, will you, Anthony?'

'Indeed, no, my lady; if a pair of chickens and a
dish of broiled ham, with strawberries from the garden, and a bowl of cream from Betty's dairy, will
content your ladyship—and this gentleman.'

'Nothing could be better, my good Anthony. But
you must not let our sudden arrival disturb you. We
have brought two coachloads of London servants, and
all they want is to be shown the way to the kitchen,
and the geography of larders, pantries, and still-
rooms, which, I remember, is rather intricate at

Hautsville.   Sir Marcus will not be able to join us
for a week.   This lady is Miss Hemsley, my husband's
niece; and this gentleman is my step-son, Mr. Everard
Lestrange.   But where is Martha ?   I shall be glad
to see her, and to settle what rooms we had best
occupy.'

Mrs. Grimshaw entered the saloon as her mistress
spoke.   She had changed her black-stuff gown for
one of stiff rustling silk, and wore a frilled-muslin
handkerchief, fastened with a diamond brooch.   Never
before had I seen her so attired.   She saluted her
mistress with a profound curtsey, and bade her
welcome to Hauteville.

My lady acknowledged her compliments somewhat
coldly, as I thought.

'How is your charge, Martha ?' she asked.   ' Your
letters have been of the briefest, and gave me little
news of him.'

I knew it was of myself she spoke, and an irresistible
impulse impelled me to approach her.   There was a
kindness in her tone which invited my confidence.
' *Here* is a friend,' I thought.

I had just lighted a pair of wax-candles, in heavy
bronze candlesticks, which stood on a writing-table
by the hearth.   With these in my hands I entered

the saloon, and carried them to the table by which
Lady Barbara had seated herself.

' O God, a ghost ! ' she cried, half-rising from her
chair, and looking at me with wide-opened eyes ; and
then sinking back into her chair, she murmured
faintly, ' You never told me he was so like.   You
should have prepared me for this, Martha.'

' My father would scarcely feel flattered by your
emotion, madam,' said Mr. Lestrange with a sneer.

' I have no secrets from your father, sir,' my lady
answered proudly ; and the gentleman's sarcastic
smile vanished as she looked at him.

' It is possible my jealousy is keener than my
father's,' he said, not without a certain significance
of tone.

Lady Barbara turned from him with an air of
supreme indifference, and addressed herself to me.

' Your face reminds me of the dead, sir ; but you
are not less welcome to me.   What is your name ? '

' Robert, madam.'

' What else ? '

' I have no other name, madam.'

' And you have never taken the pains to seek
one ?'

' No, madam.   When first I came to this house

Mrs. Grimshaw told me I was nameless.   I have asked no further questions.'

I might have added that I had been reminded not once but twenty times a week of my abandoned condition, and that such epithets as foundling, beggar, castaway, and even coarser terms of reproach, were but too familiar to me.

'Indeed!' cried my lady, with a glance at Mrs. Martha, which boded ill for that personage.   'Mrs. Grimshaw volunteered information upon a subject of which she knew little.   *She is fond of giving information.*'   This was said with a most bitter emphasis; and then, turning to me with a sweet protecting smile, Lady Barbara continued : 'Your name is Robert Ainsleigh, and you are my kinsman.   I fear you have had a somewhat desolate boyhood in this deserted house; but I placed you in the care of my old friend Anthony, because I knew you would find in him a kind friend and an accomplished tutor.'

'And I have found both, madam,' I answered promptly ; 'as good a friend as a fatherless lad ever knew, as patient and learned a master as ever earned the affection of his pupil.'

'I am glad to hear you speak so heartily,' replied my lady.   ' While I remain at Hauteville you will

live with me and my family, and it will be for yourself
to determine your future career.'

She extended her hand, and I dropped on my knee,
as I raised the fair hand to my lips.

The gentleman lounging against the chimney-
piece gave a little sarcastic laugh.

'Egad, Lady Barbara, your country cousin is a
courtier by instinct.   I warrant me he will soon eat
a toad with as good a grace as if he had hunted
tufts at the University and graduated at Leicester
House.'

I wondered at so much animosity from a stranger,
but it has been my ill-fortune in life to find more
than one bitter enemy ready-made, like this, and
to receive direst injuries from those I have never
consciously offended.

CHAPTER V.

I RISE IN THE WORLD.

IF in my childhood I had regarded Hauteville Hall as a kind of enchanted castle of fairy legend, I had still better ground for the pleasant fancy after the coming of Lady Barbara Lestrange ; for my life underwent a transformation as sudden and complete as that which befalls the prince who, after pining for years in the guise of some repulsive beast, is once more restored to his own image, and finds himself a prosperous and comely gentleman. As Robert the Nameless, dependent on an absent lady's bounty, I had endured extreme humiliation ; as Mr. Robert Ainsleigh, my lady's cousin and favourite, I was courted and flattered in a manner which at once confused and amazed me. My late tyrant, Martha Grimshaw, was of all people most obsequious ; and I perceived that, in her fear of my lady's anger, she would have stooped to any degradation in order to conciliate me. I received her advances with supreme coldness, and took occasion to inform her that she had nothing to fear from my malice or to hope from my regard.

'It was my misfortune to live with you for ten years,' I said; 'and it is difficult for any man to blot out the memory of so long a period; but, so far as it is possible, I will forget the slights you have inflicted upon me, and the petty spite which has influenced your conduct towards me from the day of our first meeting. Your husband's kindness to me has, however, been as unvarying as your own harshness, and you may be secure that my respect for him will prevent me from injuring you.'

Mrs. Grimshaw's dull gray eye shone with a pale fire as she answered me.

'I am much beholden to you, sir,' she said in slow measured tones, 'that you should condescend so far as to refrain from injuring me in the opinion of my mistress, whose last caprice inclines her to patronize you. You are as yet a stranger to the whims and humours of a fine lady, and I scarce wonder that your sudden elevation has turned your head. It is a new thing for a penniless dependent to be raised from the society of such low persons as my husband and myself to the company of an earl's daughter and an ambassador's son; but I would have you remember that it is easier to come downstairs than to go upwards, and that you may some day find yourself turned out of doors, as Mr. Roderick Ainsleigh was before you.'

'My father was not turned out of doors!' I cried angrily.

'Your father! Who gave you an earl's nephew for your father? Pray where is your certificate of birth, or your mother's marriage lines? You are quick to boast of your father; and I doubt not, if he has bequeathed you his face, you have inherited his wicked heart also.'

'Why do you malign him?' I exclaimed; 'he never can have injured you.'

'Of course not,' cried Mrs. Grimshaw bitterly; 'what should there be in common between low-born dirt like me and such a gentleman as that? Why, nothing. But I tell you this, Robert Ainsleigh— since it pleases you to borrow a bad man's name— your father brought sorrow wherever he came, and there were few who looked on his face who did not live to rue having seen it.'

The inconsequence of this speech mystified me,

but I did not question Mrs. Grimshaw, who departed malevolent as ever—more malevolent, if possible, since I had repudiated her civilities.

In my new phase of existence, however, I saw but little of the severe Martha. For me there was to be no more of Mr. Whitefield's Calvinistic discourse, no more tracts of alarming import, no more prim one-o'clock dinners in the oak parlour, no more silent comfortless meals beneath the gaze of my persecutor.

From the little whitewashed chamber at the top of a narrow wooden staircase, where I had slept ever since my first coming to Hauteville Hall, I found myself transferred to an airy and spacious tapestried apartment over the library, with an oriel window looking on the Italian garden. A tailor from Warborough came to take my orders for several suits of the prevailing fashion, and Lady Barbara herself assisted me to select patterns and colours, while Mr. Snip waited respectfully with his pattern-book across his arm. My mornings were still given to the classics with my kind master, Anthony Grimshaw; but after we had read an act of a Greek tragedy, or the funeral oration of Pericles, or a dozen pages of Tacitus, my tutor and I parted company; and unless

I made it my business to join him as he took his after-dinner pipe on the terrace, we saw no more of each other till the next day. In short, I was now a gentleman, and my sphere was the drawing-room, where I sat by Lady Barbara's tambour-frame, or hung over Miss Hemsley's harpsichord, as if I had been to the manner born. How shall I describe the kindness of my kinswoman, who, having chosen to assume the care of my fortunes, was determined to fufil her duty to the uttermost!

'It seems cruel to have left you so long to languish in this lonely place,' she said, during our first *tête-à-tête;* 'but I could not get Sir Marcus away from Madrid, and it would have seemed ungracious to leave him; so I waited, almost hoping for some breach between England and Spain, in order to bring about my husband's recall. And then the years slipped by so quickly. I knew Anthony would be kind to you, and I did not think Martha would be unkind, which I fear she was, though you refuse to admit as much. In short, dear cousin, believe me, I was not so cruel as I must needs have seemed.'

'You never seemed to me anything but my bountiful benefactress and friend,' I replied; 'I knew that I owed everything to you, and must have perished but for your charity.'

'No, Robert, I will not have that word.'

'Nay, dear madam, there is no other fits your goodness.'

And again my lady gave me her hand, which I once more raised to my lips in grateful homage.

I was now installed as one of the family, with as little sense of dependence as it is possible for a dependent to feel.

I was agreeably surprised by the conduct of Mr. Lestrange, who treated me with a cordiality which I was far from expecting to receive from him, after his supercilious tone on the night of our first meeting. He was something of a fop and fine gentleman ; but pronounced himself, nevertheless, delighted with the park and woods, the noble trout-stream which intersected the estate, and in which I was able to show him the deeps and shallows, the shadowy inlets where his fly might do most execution, and the reedy margins where he might be sure of a gigantic jack. He suffered me to do the honours of Hauteville, and entertained me agreeably with his own adventures at home and abroad, which he was never tired of relating. I discovered by and by that this gentleman, who was yet on the sunny side of his twenty-seventh birthday, was past-master of the knowledge of evil, and had long outlived his abhorrence of the vices and his respect for the virtues of his fellow-men.

I did not, however, make this discovery immediately, being too much unused to the society of fine gentlemen, and to the world in general, to be a skilled observer. Little by little these things revealed themselves to me; and I had been some months in Mr. Everard's company before I learned rightly to estimate his civilities or to appreciate his value.

His father arrived at the Hall within a week of Lady Barbara's advent; and I was presented to that important personage with all due ceremony. He received me with a somewhat cold courtesy, and I was quick to discover that my presence gave him little pleasure. Toleration was, evidently, all I must expect from him; but the kindness of my benefactress would have compensated me for worse treatment from Sir Marcus; and while I took care not to intrude myself upon that gentleman, I rigidly refrained from any attempt to conciliate his good graces. My grateful affection for my protectress might be misinterpreted; for that I cared little; but I was determined to eat no toads for Sir Marcus Lestrange.

Happily for me, however, the diplomatist was by
no means a domestic character. He spent the greater
part of his day in his study, and of an evening played
piquet with my lady in her dressing-room, while
Everard Lestrange, Miss Hemsley, and myself amused
ourselves in the saloon, or strolled on the terrace and
in the garden. He paid numerous visits to the seats
of the neighbouring nobility and gentry, travelling
sometimes as many as thirty miles to a dinner, and
altogether troubled us but little with his company.
He was an elegant and accomplished gentleman, of
about fifty years of age, in person much resembling
his only son, but of more perfect although colder
manners. Between himself and Everard there obtained a stately politeness which did not betoken
a very warm affection. It was rather the manner
of skilled fencers on guard than of a father
and son. My lady told me in confidence that
Sir Marcus desired to see his son united in marriage with Dorothea, or Dora, Hemsley, not only
the most amiable of women, but a considerable
fortune.

' Whether this will ever come to pass I know not,'
she said in conclusion ; ' but I am bound to assist my
husband's projects. Dora is a sweet girl, and my

only fear is that Everard should prove unworthy of her.'

'They are not betrothed to each other, are they, madam?' I asked, perhaps more anxiously than the circumstances warranted.

'No, there has been no formal betrothal; but Dora can hardly be ignorant of her uncle's wish. She was left an orphan five years ago, and since that time has lived with me. I do not know what I should do without her. I have no children of my own, you see, Robert. There is a little grave in Spain that I cannot think of at this day without a heartache, though it is fifteen years old; but no child of mine lived to call me mother. Yes, Dora is very dear to me,' she added, abruptly changing the subject.

This confidence occurred within a week of Lady Barbara's arrival. In after-days, when I had suffered a bitter pain and languished under the burden of a secret sorrow, I could not help thinking that my benefactress had told me these things thus early in order that no peril might arise from my daily companionship with Dora Hemsley. But there is one disease against which antidotes and preventives are administered in vain, and from this cruel fever I was doomed to suffer.

CHAPTER VI.

I FALL IN LOVE.

DURING one of our earliest rambles in Hauteville Woods, I introduced Mr. Everard Lestrange to the warrener's lodge, where the travelled gentleman soon contrived to make himself agreeable to honest Dame Hawker and my sweet Margery, who had blossomed into rare beauty in the calm solitude of her woodland home. She was but just seventeen years of age, slim and graceful as the young fawns which had frisked around her and eaten from her rosy palm. Her beauty was that of a true wood-nymph, and had nothing in common with Dorothea Hemsley's fair loveliness. Margery's skin was a pale olive, charmingly relieved by the deep crimson of cheeks and lips. Her eyes were hazel-brown, large, bright, and sparkling with the innocent viva-city of a pure and fearless soul; her hair also a rich nut-brown, tinged with gold—waving rippling hair,

which defied her girlish vanity when she would fain
have pinned and pinched it into some semblance
of the two or three fashionable heads she saw at
church.

I had happened to tell my new acquaintance that
Jack Hawker was an excellent angler, and his
daughter skilled in the fabrication of a famous
trout-fly, whereupon Mr. Lestrange expressed himself eager to see my foster-father.

'A very bower of Arcadia!' he cried, as we
approached the dear old white-walled cottage. 'And
so this is where you were reared? I declare,
Ainsleigh, you were a lucky dog to have a scoundrel
for your father.'

'Scoundrel or no scoundrel, as he was my father
I would rather you called him no hard names,' I
answered somewhat sullenly; for I had no idea of
suffering this gentleman to throw dirt at Roderick
Ainsleigh's grave.

We found the cottage tenantless. Jack Hawker
was doubtless absent on his rounds, and it was
market-day at Warborough, whither my foster-
mother went every week to make her purchases,
and dispose of small produce in the way of honey
and eggs, and vegetables from the fertile garden.

The doors being all opened, in the sultry midsummer weather, we went into the kitchen, whence we beheld as fair a vision as painter ever perpetuated by the work of his brush.

At the end of a narrow garden-path, overarched by the straggling boughs of elder, quince, and hazel, stood Margery, in the centre of a little grass-plot, with the sunshine on her loose uncovered hair and light chintz petticoat. She was feeding her poultry, which swarmed eagerly round her, and did sturdy battle amongst themselves for the barley which her pretty hands shook down on them from a well-filled sieve. So busily was she occupied as not to be aware of our approach till we stood within a few yards of her; and then it was a pretty sight to see her bashfulness and sweet blushing confusion when she glanced suddenly upward and perceived us watching her.

She came and shook me by the hand, and dropped a low curtsey to my companion. Her manner towards myself had much changed during the last year. She was no longer the familiar foster-sister who had been wont to hold up her rosy lips to receive the fraternal kiss, but a bashful maiden, whose eyelids drooped when we met, and

from whom I had sometimes trouble to extort more
than murmured monosyllabic replies to my talk,
yet who would by fits and starts be vivacious and
animated, playful and capricious, as some forest
elf.

This I took to be the natural shyness of maiden-
hood, that tender early dawn of life in which a
woman is wholly surprised and half-ashamed to
find herself beautiful and admired.

I requested Margery to show us some golden
pheasants of her own rearing, the feathers of which
were of inestimable value to the angler; and she
conducted us to a roomy, rough wire cage, em-
bosomed among roses and seringa, proud to exhibit
her favourites.

After these had been duly admired, Mr. Lestrange
complained of thirst, and I begged a bowl of milk
for him; whereon Margery led us to her mother's
dairy, a cool shadowy chamber paved with stone,
and odorous with the perfume of eglantine and
honeysuckle.

Here she made us welcome to such refreshment
as the place could offer, and we loitered for some
time drinking milk and eating cheesecakes of a
substantial quality. I was surprised to discover

how quickly Everard Lestrange made himself agreeable to the rustic girl, contriving speedily to engage her in familiar conversation, and to amuse her by his talk of London, that marvellous city of which she knew less than she knew of fairyland.

We bade Margery good-bye, after she had promised to make us some flies against our next visit; and as we walked away from the cottage, my companion complimented me upon my good fortune in owning so lovely a foster-sister.

'Methinks thou wert born under a lucky star, Robert,' cried the gentleman, in that affected style which I found afterwards to obtain among young men of his class.

'I do not know what you mean by good luck,' I replied. 'I love my foster-sister dearly; but I consider it no special good fortune that she should have grown up so handsome. Indeed, I doubt if beauty is the best of gifts for a cottager's daughter.'

'Spoken like a true disciple of the saintly Noggers of Brewer's Yard, Warborough,' cried Mr. Lestrange with a sneer. 'Beauty is a delusion and a snare, brother Jumper,—do you jump in Brewer's Yard meeting-house, by the way, or do you belong to the quieter folks who only preach and pray?—

yea verily, comeliness of visage is but a snare to
the wicked and a bait for fools; and 'tis better to
be a flat-faced and pug-nosed damsel than a bright
woodland siren, with great hazel eyes, in which
the sunshine plays at bo-peep, and lips like ripe
cherries.'

I did not care to hear these florid compliments;
and though at this time I knew but little of
Everard Lestrange, I resolved that I would take
him to Jack Hawker's cottage as seldom as possible.

'One would think, by your raptures, you had
fallen in love with my pretty sister,' I said, somewhat coldly.

'Why, thou simplest of rustics, such raptures are
the common language with a man of the world where
women are in question. We think and talk of them
in hyperbole, and the homeliest among them is angel
or goddess before marriage. It is only after the
honeymoon that we descend to the regions of fact,
and confess that Lesbia is a slattern and Marcella a
scold. As for your pretty woodland nymph yonder,
it would fare ill with me should I lose my heart in
that quarter; for so surely as I am a skilled observer
of womankind, hers is already forfeited.'

'To whom, pray?'

'To you, Mr. Demure; to you, who pretend to be unconscious of your power. Did you mark how ready the sly puss was to converse with me, and how bravely her beautiful eyes met mine, stranger as I am? But at a word from you the dark lashes droop, and the gipsy face reddens with a sudden blush. I would forfeit my chances of favour with the Duke of Newcastle to be in your shoes, were I free to wish.'

I understood these last words to allude to his relations with Miss Hemsley. I hastened to assure him that he was mistaken as to Margery's sentiments.

'We regard each other as brother and sister, but no more,' I said. 'I have watched her cradle many a day when I was little more than a baby myself. We were together for nearly eight years,—constant playfellows and companions,—and the friendship between us has never been interrupted.'

'And is that any reason she should not love you?'

'The strongest. I don't believe that love is ever born of custom and affection. 'Tis the sudden sight of a sweet strange face that first tells a man he has a heart.'

Mr. Lestrange stared hard at me, and I felt my cheeks crimson under his gaze.

'And what sweet strange face has Mr. Ainsleigh seen of late that has made him so wise?' he demanded with a sneer.

'I speak of love in the abstract,' I answered, and hastily changed the conversation; but on several occasions after this I caught Everard Lestrange watching my face with a somewhat unfriendly expression upon his own.

'The sudden sight of a sweet strange face.' The words had escaped me unawares, and they hinted at a secret scarce known to myself. 'Twas the pale, white-rose face of Dorothea Hemsley that was in my mind.

And she was to marry this cynical worldling, with his sneers and affectations, because she had a fortune, and could advance her cousin's prospects! Remote and impossible a creature as she must ever be for me, I could but lament that family interests should assign her to so unfitting a partner; and I feared that so gentle a nature would never sustain any contest with the will of others, should the young lady's inclinations be opposed to the match.

This I had some reason to conclude was the case.

I had seen Miss Hemsley and her suitor together, and had seen on her part an avoidance which was something more than maiden modesty. She was polite and gentle in her demeanour towards her cousin, as she was to the lowest servant in the house; but I observed that she artfully eluded all occasions of being alone with him. In order to do this she sometimes invited my companionship, and I was thus at an early stage of our acquaintance drawn into a dangerous intimacy with her. She volunteered to teach me chess, and instructed me in the performance of the simple symphonies and accompaniments to two or three easy bass songs by Handel and Gluck.

That these favours bestowed on me were displeasing to Mr. Lestrange, I had, even at this period, no doubt; but he contrived to conceal his anger, and treated his cousin and myself with perfect amiability.

I found it no easy matter to keep my lady's step-son from the warrener's lodge, where he managed to make himself vastly agreeable to simple Jack Hawker and his simple wife, who thought this town-bred gentleman the most perfect specimen of courtesy and good-manners. Margery brightened at our coming, and seemed always alike delighted to receive us; nor was I well pleased to perceive the rapid progress which Mr. Lestrange appeared to make in her favour, since I had by this time become acquainted with the loose ideas and contemptuous opinions which he entertained of all womankind, from the duchesses whose favours he hinted at to the dairy-maids whose ruin he boasted. Towards me my foster-sister's manner was shyer and more subdued every time we met, but with Everard Lestrange she gossipped and laughed with perfect freedom.

This gentleman often rallied us upon our secret attachment, and his jests covered the poor girl with blushes and confusion, much to the amusement of Jack Hawker, who saw no reason why his daughter should be an unworthy alliance for Lady Barbara's penniless protégé. I had told my old friends at the warrener's lodge nothing of my cousinship with the mistress of Hauteville, and they still regarded me as a nameless waif, dependent on the charity of my noble benefactress.

I did not, however, continue to afford Mr. Lestrange occasion for his broadly expressed insinuations, which were embarassing to Margery, and to the last degree painful to myself. As the summer advanced I spent less time in the woods, and left my lady's stepson to go fishing by himself, while I read with Lady Barbara and Miss Hemsley in the Hauteville library. My benefactress was well pleased to resume her studious habits, and we formed a little company of students, with Anthony Grimshaw for our preceptor. Together we read Virgil, Dante, and Tasso, and my lady was so good as to express herself much pleased with my progress as a linguist.

'The dear boy has a rare talent for languages,' said my gratified master, 'and we have worked hard at the cultivation of foreign tongues, which of all accomplishments is the most valuable for a man who has to make his way in the world. For Greek and Latin I will match Robert against any lad of his age; he knows Italian thoroughly, and is a fair Frenchman; and he has, moreover, a smattering of Sanscrit, which may some day be useful to him.'

'I doubt whether his knowledge of Sanscrit will ever serve him for much,' my lady answered, smiling, 'unless he should have a fancy for extending his travels as far as the court of the Great Mogul, or should turn Jesuit missionary and strive to convert the heathens of Birmah or Thibet. But

the habit of study is a good one, and I am proud to
think my cousin has been so diligent a pupil.'

While I did my best to improve Miss Hemsley's
Italian, which was far from equal to the obscurities
of Dante, that young lady was so kind as to
instruct me in the Spanish tongue, of which she
had made herself mistress during her five-years'
residence at Madrid. With this gentle instructress
I speedily mastered the soft, sleepy syllables of that
mellifluous language, and read *Don Quixote* in the
original before our studies were concluded.

For these studies Mr. Lestrange did not scruple
to avow his contempt. He quoted Molière's
Femmes Savantes, and christened my lady Bélise,
and Dora Hemsley Armande. He spoke of us as
the Hauteville Blue-stocking Club, and suggested
that we should invite Lord Lyttleton and Mrs.
Montague to join the party.

I, for my part, was too happy to heed his sneers;
days, weeks, and months slipped by, and I well-nigh
forgot that I had ever been solitary in that house
where my life was now so pleasant. My acquaintance with Dora Hemsley had ripened into friendship. She talked to me of my lonely boyhood,
of her own happy youth, watched over by beloved

parents, and of the bitter grief that fell upon her
with the loss of them. She told me of Lady
Barbara's tender kindness, and of the affection
which had gone so far to supply the place of the
lost. But of her uncle's desire to bring about a
marriage between herself and his son she never
spoke; nor was she ever betrayed into expressing
any opinion respecting Everard Lestrange. One
day when Everard and she had been by chance
alone together for some minutes, I surprised her in
tears. Mr. Lestrange quitted the room by one door
as I entered by another, and I found Dora seated on
one of the window-seats, with her arms resting on
the broad stone sill, and her head and face hidden
in her clasped hands. I saw the tears trickling
between the slender fingers, and had not sufficient
command of myself to refrain from questioning her.

'Dear Miss Hemsley,' I cried, 'for God's sake
tell me what distresses you!'

She lifted her head and turned her sweet face
towards me, bathed in tears.

'That I can tell to no one,' she answered; 'I
have my secret troubles to bear, Mr. Ainsleigh,
though I am but just eighteen years of age; and I
must endure them with patience.'

I knelt at her feet, and begged her to believe that if the sacrifice of my life could have served her I would have freely given it. She turned her tearful eyes towards me.

'Yes, Robert,' she said, 'I think you would do much to save me from sorrow. But you cannot. I must bear my burden.'

The sound of my Christian name spoken by her lips thrilled my soul like a strange sweet music. But at the same moment there came another sound that startled me. 'Twas the stealthy opening of a door. I looked up and saw Mr. Lestrange peering in at us through a narrow opening, from the doorway by which I had seen him leave the room. Our eyes met, and he clapped-to the door; but in that one instant I had seen the expression of his face, and never did I behold more malignity upon the human countenance.

I would willingly have pressed Miss Hemsley further, but she entreated me to refrain, and I left her, sore distressed by her grief, and only able to guess at its cause.

'Everard Lestrange has been urging his suit with her,' I thought; ''tis clear she does not love him.'

And then I suffered my fancy to beguile me with a bright dream of what might have been if I had not been a penniless dependent, and Miss Hemsley a fortune; and I cursed the wealth which made an impassable barrier between us.

CHAPTER VII.

HOW I BECAME AN ORPHAN.

I WAS pacing the long corridor of the upper story in a despondent frame of mind, when the door of my lady's dressing-room opened, and Mrs. Grimshaw emerged, more than usually sour of visage.

'You are wanted by my lady,' she said on seeing me. 'I have been urging upon her that such an idle life as you are leading is not the way to fit a young man for earning his livelihood, and she is so good as to acknowledge the wisdom of my remarks.'

'You are very obliging with advice that has not been invited,' I answered; 'but since I doubt if you have ever wished me well, I should be grateful if you would abstain from all interference with my affairs.'

I knew that whatever influence this woman brought to bear upon my fate would be of an adverse nature, and I could not patiently brook her

tone of patronage and superiority. She gave me a
malignant glance, muttered something about a beggar on horseback, and passed on, while I went to
Lady Barbara's dressing-room, a spacious and
cheerful apartment, hung with prints and chalk
drawings, and furnished with japanned cabinets
containing shells, dried flowers, Indian china, and
many valuable curios of the monster tribe. It was
the room my lady had occupied as a girl, and which
she preferred to any other apartment at Hauteville.
A large embroidered screen in tent-stitch, repre-
senting the meeting of Joseph and his brethren,
testified to her girlish industry; and half a dozen
dogs of the pug species sprawling on a rug before
the sunniest of the windows, revealed the hobby
of her childless matronhood.

She was writing as I entered, but closed her desk
immediately, and looked up at me with an affectionate smile.

'Sit you down here, Robert,' she said, pointing
to a stool at her feet; and I seated myself there,
and took the hand which she offered me. Thus
grouped, we seemed like mother and son.

'Robert,' she began presently, 'I think you know
that I love you.'

'Yes, indeed, dear madam; and your affection has made me very happy.'

'Will you cease to believe in that affection if I should be obliged to make you unhappy?'

'I cannot believe that you will ever act unkindly.'

'Not willingly, Robert, God knows. But you remember what Shakespeare makes his Hamlet say: we must sometimes "be cruel, only to be kind." Dear boy, I think we have all been too happy here; you and I and Dora Hemsley. Do you remember what I told you about Dora when we first came?'

'I am not likely to forget it,' I answered gloomily.

'It was my manner of warning you, Robert. I cannot thwart my husband's wishes with reference to his niece and ward; I cannot, Robert, even to serve you. He was very generous when I asked leave to adopt you, poor orphan child; and it would ill repay his goodness if you became the instrument to bring about the disappointment of his favourite scheme. He has set his heart upon his son's marriage with Dora, and it must take place; or, at least, you and I must do nothing to prevent it.'

'God forbid it should ever come to pass!' I cried.

'Why, Robert, have you anything to say against Everard Lestrange?'

'Not much, except that I do not like him; and I can scarce tell you wherefore. *Non amo te, Sabidi, nec possum dicere quare*—'

'Heavens, how like that was said to your father! Ah, Robert, I doubt you inherit his headstrong, impetuous disposition.'

I smiled, remembering how quiet and submissive had been my youth; and yet I was inclined to doubt whether under certain exceptional circumstances a fiery spirit, to which I was at present a stranger, might not reveal himself as my master. Surely if for every man there watches and prays a good angel, so each has his familiar demon, an invisible director stronger than himself, who leads him where he would not go, and urges him to deeds he would fain leave undone.

'Robert,' said my benefactress suddenly, after a little pause, 'I have watched you and Dora together, and I think it would be well for the peace, nay, indeed, for the honour of both, that you should part.'

'I am ready, madam,' cried I, springing to my feet with a start. 'I know that there is a gulf between that bright angel and me. Send me away this day—this minute. I am ready to go.'

I dashed a tear from my eyes as I spoke. My lady watched me with a sad, perplexed face.

' O Robert,' she cried, ' has it come to this?'

' Yes,' I answered. ' Your warning has been forgotten; I love her. I will not come between your stepson and his fortune. I love her; but I am not so base a viper as to sting the breast that has warmed and sheltered me. I will not bring trouble on you, dear lady. From these lips Dora Hemsley shall never hear that she is beloved. O, let me go; let me leave this dear place, where for the last few months I have tasted such dangerous, such fatal happiness.'

' Yes, Robert, you must go. It will be wisest and best that you should begin life at once; and your future will be my care, dear boy, do not doubt that. And so my gentle Dora has won your heart? 'Tis but a boy's love,. a brief fever, more easily cured than you can believe while the disease rages. But do you know, Robert, that I have heard of another passion of yours?'

'How, madam?'

'That pretty brown-eyed girl at the warrener's lodge, Margery Hawker—what of her, Robert?'

'She is my foster-sister, and as dear to me as ever sister was to brother. Who told you she was more than that, Lady Barbara?'

'I have been *told* nothing; but I have had hints.'

'Shame on the hinters, madam! People who mean well can afford to speak plainly. I can guess who is at the bottom of this.'

'Perhaps there are more than you think, Robert. Do not be so angry. If you have pledged your heart to poor little Margery, keep your faith with her. Better to have a peasant-girl for your wife, than a guilty conscience and the bitter memory of having broken an honest woman's heart.'

'I swear to you, dear madam, that Margery has never been more to me than my foster-sister, and never will be. I know that she is beautiful— lovelier than Miss Hemsley, even; but she has never touched my heart, as one look of that young lady's touched me on the first night of her coming here. I think there must be some element of magic in such spells, innocent as they seem.'

'I cannot doubt you when you speak so boldly. But O, Robert, let there be no broken hearts—no ruined lives. There has been too much of that already.'

I looked at her wonderingly, and she answered my inquiring glance.

'Your father's heart and mine, Robert—your father's life and mine—both broken, both ruined, for want of a little more candour, a little more patience, a little more constancy. I loved him so dearly! Yes, that is why you are as dear to me as ever only son was to doting mother. I cannot tell you how happy we were as boy and girl together, or how devoted he seemed to me. I know that in those days he was all truth, all goodness. There was no hidden evil in that proud young heart. He had his faults, perhaps, but they were the failings of a knight-errant. Who can say that Sir Philip Sidney was faultless? and we know that Raleigh was a sinner. His errors were ever those of a great mind. O God, how easy it is for me to pardon and pity him now; I who was so unforgiving then, when my pardon might have saved him! When he came from the University I thought him changed, and there was one about me who took care to call my attention to the change, and by-and-by to assign a cause for it. Martha Peyton, now Martha Grimshaw, my conscientious, confidential, trustworthy maid, discovered an incipient intrigue of my cousin's, and brought me speedy news of it. Mr. Ainsleigh was always hanging about Parson Lester's vicarage, she told me. Mr. Lester was a hunting-parson, renowned for his knowledge of horses and his veterinary skill, and this might fairly be the magnet that drew Roderick to his house. But my confidential maid would not have me think this. Mr. Lester had an only daughter, a pretty, empty-headed girl, and Martha hinted that it was for her sake my cousin haunted the vicarage. I had seen the girl at church, and had invited her to tea in my dressing-room, and given her a cast-off gown now and then, to the aggravation of my confidential Martha, who was inclined to be jealous of intruders. I knew that Amelia Lester was weak, and frivolous, and pretty, and I believed my informant. I had no civil word for my cousin after this, and would hear neither explanations nor apologies, which at first he fain would have made. The breach grew wider day by day. O Robert, I was madly, wickedly jealous. I hated my rival, my false lover, myself, the whole world. One day I met Roderick and Amelia together

in the park, the girl simpering and blushing under
her hat, my cousin with the conqueror's easy, self-
satisfied air. He did not even blush on meeting me,
but passed me by with a cool nod and smile of defiance, while Miss Amelia dropped me a low curtsey,
with her eyes cast modestly to the ground. After
this meeting I scarcely deigned to speak to my cousin,
and suffered unspeakable torments with a haughty
countenance. Women have a genius for self-torture.
I would have given worlds to bring Roderick to my
feet, to be assured that I alone was beloved by him.
Yet I obstinately repelled his advances, and neglected every opportunity of reconciliation.'

'Your mind had been poisoned, dear madam,' I
said; for I knew but too well Mrs. Grimshaw's hard,
cruel nature, and could now perceive that her hatred
was a heritage that came to me from my father,
whom she had pursued with that fury which the
poets tell us to be worse than the hate of hell.

'Yes, my mind had been poisoned,' replied my
lady; 'my confidante, from pure conscientiousness,
no doubt—but there are no people can wound like
these conscientious friends—kept me informed of my
cousin's doings. His visits to the vicarage were
notorious. Miss Lester had boasted everywhere of

her conquest. 'Everywhere' is a vague word; but I was too angry, too miserable, to insist upon particulars. And then, was I not heiress of Hauteville? and should my cousin affect the most ardent devotion, how could I believe him? My confidante took occasion to remind me of my wealth; these prudent people have such sordid notions. Had I known the world then as I know it now, Robert, I should have valued your father so much the more for the pride that held him aloof from me after my numerous repulses had chilled and wounded him. But I believed myself deserted and betrayed for a person whom I considered my inferior; and when my father's anger was aroused by the discovery of certain debts which Roderick had concealed from him, I made no attempt to act as peacemaker. Then came a long and stormy interview, which resulted in my cousin's abrupt departure from Hauteville, never again to sleep beneath this roof. He went without a word of farewell. My father declared he would return, and I too hoped long in the face of despair. O Robert, for me those were the days of retribution. What a long heart-sickness, what a weary agony! For a year I listened and watched for Roderick Ainsleigh's return. Every sound of a horse's hoofs in the distance, every sudden stroke of the great bell, every messenger or letter-carrier who came to this old place, raised hope that was awakened only to be disappointed. My confidential maid fell ill of the small-pox soon after my cousin's departure, but that fatal malady passed me by, though I would fain have courted any death-stroke. Within six months of Roderick's disappearance Amelia Lester left her father's house, secretly, as it was rumoured, though the parson affected to know where she was. She had gone to some relations in Somersetshire, he said, and as no one but he had any right to be angry, the assertion was suffered to pass unchallenged; except by Martha Peyton, who contrived to extort the truth from a servant at the vicarage. The young lady had been missing one morning, and the father had raged and stormed for a while, and then had cursed her for a worthless hussy, saying that no doubt she had run after Roderick Ainsleigh, about whom her head had been turned for the last three years. This was the story Martha told me, and she wanted to bring the vicarage servant to confirm it. I told her I required no confirmation of my cousin's baseness, and that she need trouble herself no more about my affairs. But the blow struck none the less severely because I was too proud to show the pain. I was so steeped in misery, that my father's sudden death shocked me much less than it would have done at any other time; and when it was suggested that I should visit an aunt in London, I consented listlessly, with some faint sense of relief in the idea of leaving Hauteville.'

'And there came no tidings of my father, even on the death of his benefactor?'

'No; but I have since had reason to believe that Roderick attended his uncle's funeral. A figure in a black cloak appeared among the group around the mausoleum in the park. The funeral was celebrated at night, and the stranger, who kept aloof from the rest of the mourners, drew upon himself the notice of the torch-bearers. One of these afterwards declared that he had seen either Mr. Ainsleigh or his ghost.'

'And did you never see him again, Lady Barbara?'

'Never, Robert, never. No sign reached me to tell if he were still amongst the living. I will not enter into the manifold reasons that prompted my marriage, which was not in any sense a love-match. Sir Marcus knew that I had no heart to give, and was content to accept my esteem and obedience. Nor have either of us, I believe, had reason to repent our union. Sir Marcus has ever proved a kind and indulgent husband, and my life has been happier than that of many a woman who marries for love. But I have not forgotten my girlhood, Robert, and all my old hopes and dreams and troubles come back to me when I look upon your face.'

She opened her desk and handed me an oval morocco case, containing a miniature. I recognised the countenance I had seen in the oil-painting shown me by Anthony Grimshaw, that dark strongly-marked face which bore so close a resemblance in feature and complexion to my own.

'You grow more like him every day,' said my lady. 'That miniature was his only gift to me. 'Twas painted before doubt or anger had arisen between us.'

'And did you never hear more of him, madam?'

'Yes, Robert. Six months after my marriage a letter reached me—a letter from my cousin Roderick. It was long and wild, telling me how I had been beloved, and how my coldness had angered that proud heart. I have the letter in this desk, but every word of it is burnt into my memory, in-effaceable as the graver's work upon metal. "If I could not be happy with her I loved, I could at least be wretched with one who loved me," he wrote;

H 2

"and I found a faithful creature, Barbara, who was gladder to unite herself to my broken fortunes than a wiser woman would have been to follow a better man."   And then my poor proud Roderick went on to confess that he had fallen very low, so low that his sole hope for the partner of his wretchedness rested on my compassion.   "And you showed a great contempt for this poor creature once, Barbara," he added.'

'He had married the parson's daughter, then ?'

'Ay, Robert, she was the sharer of his sorrows.'

'Will you let me see my father's letter, madam ?'

My lady hesitated for some moments, and then took the paper from a secret drawer of her desk.

'I know not whether I am wise, Robert,' she said, 'but perhaps it is best you should learn all that I can tell you.'

She handed me the letter, written on tavern paper, in a bold, clear penmanship, which was not without some family resemblance to my own.

Together Lady Barbara and I read the faded lines:

'I stood amongst the crowd that watched your wedding, cousin,' continued the writer, 'as I had watched unseen on a former occasion.   I needed not

the confirmation of that ambitious alliance to prove
that you had never loved me.   You but yielded to
your father's wish that his sister's son should share
his daughter's fortune, and were but too glad to
find an excuse for breaking my heart.   Great
Heaven, what a wretch am I to reproach you!—a
tavern-haunting, plotting reprobate to dare upbraid
my lord ambassador's lady because she is cold and
cruel, and severed from me by a gulf that fate, or
her pride, or my folly has dug between us!   Ah,
Barbara, I am very tired of this wearisome struggle,
this muddled dream of a drunkard, called life.   If
I should make a sudden sinful end of it, wouldst
thou have pity on a poor faithful wretch starving
in a lodging near St. Bride's Church, Fleet Street?
'Tis at a dyer's, 17, Monk's Alley, a narrow court
betwixt the church and the Temple—hard for a fine
lady's footman to find, but not beyond the ken of
charity.   Go to her soon, Barbara Lestrange, if
thou wouldst have one poor woman and her infant
snatched from the many who perish unknown under
the gracious sway of our beneficent Hanoverian
ruler.   A helpless woman and an infant cry to you,
cousin.   The child is of your own blood.   But the
messenger waits, and my paper will hold no more.

I bribe him with my last sixpence to carry this letter to St. James's Square. God grant he may be faithful! God grant Amelia and my child may find you kind! 'Tis perhaps the last prayer of your wretched humble servant,

'RODERICK AINSLEIGH.

'ROSE AND CROWN TAVERN, SOHO,
   ' *November*, 15*th*, 1731.

'N.B.—Inquire for Mrs. Adams. I have spared the pride of my family, and am only known to the companions of my poverty as Robert Adams.'

'As our evil fortune would have it—and there seemed ever to interpose a cruel fate between Roderick and me—I was away from London when this letter was brought; and the shabbiness of the messenger bespeaking no respect from the porter who received it, the poor letter was laid aside with bills and petitions, and other insignificant papers, to await my return. The date of my cousin's appeal was a week old when I received it, and, prompt as I was to seek Monk's Alley, I was too late to see him whose face I so longed to look upon once more. I found only a dying woman—the very ghost of that vain village beauty whom I had known as Amelia

Lester—and a sickly child. This poor wretched soul
was too far gone in fever to recognise me. She
raved deliriously of her Roderick, and it was piteous
to hear her imploring him to come back. Even in
this dying state she tried to nourish her child, until
the dyer's wife, a decent, charitable creature, who had
received no rent for many weeks, took the babe into
her care. For a week your mother lingered, Robert,
and I visited her daily, and gave her such succour as
was possible. She was past cure when I found her.'

'And had my father deserted her?'

'No, Robert. From the dyer's wife I learned
that your father had ever been kind to his companion
in misery. He had come home intoxicated sometimes, roaring tipsy songs about wine and women,
but had never been harsh to the poor soul, who
watched and waited for him and loved him with
unchanging fidelity. Sometimes he had stayed
at home gloomy and brooding for days together.
The woman believed that he had lived by writing
political pamphlets for the booksellers. Once he
had written something treasonable, and had been
threatened with a prosecution, and had lain in
hiding for several weeks. For a year and a half he
had lodged in this mean, stifling alley, in this bare,

wretched garret, while all Hauteville, of which he
was to have been master, lay dark and empty and
desolate for want of him.   There never was a stable-
help in my father's service lodged so meanly as his
once-beloved nephew. Ah, Robert, the thought of
this stung me to the quick.   " Let him come back,
and I will share my fortune with him," I said to
myself, forgetting that my fortune was no longer
mine alone, and that I had given another the right
to counsel, if not to dictate, my disposal of it.'

' And he never came back?' I asked breathlessly.

' Never. He had been missing a week when I
found Amelia. He must have disappeared on the
very night when his letter to me was written. But
the dyer's wife was not alarmed. He had often
absented himself for two or three days at a time, it
appeared. Yet 'twas strange, she owned, so kind
a gentleman should desert a dying woman. He
might have been taken to some prison, for debt, or
libel, or treason. I caused the lists of every prison
in London to be examined, but did not find my
cousin.

' I sent my agent to the booksellers to inquire for
such a pamphlet-writer. One among them knew
him well as Mr. Adams of Monk's Alley, and had

given him frequent employment, but had of late found no work for him. The town was beginning to tire of patriotism spiced with treason ; Church and State had been reviled and ridiculed till not a rag was left from which to spin an essay. If a new Butler had arisen to write a new *Hudibras*, the book would scarce have sold. I knew by this that Roderick's means of livelihood had failed him before he had written to me ; and, taking this in conjunction with that hint of a sudden sinful end to his wretchedness, I could but fear that my unhappy cousin had destroyed himself.'

' Was he so miserable as to commit that sin ?'

' No, Robert, he did not perish by his own hand; yet I know not if his end were less sinful. He fell in a midnight brawl at the tavern where his letter was written, and on the very night on which it was dated—a most wretched, profligate haunt near Soho Square. He had been buried ten days when my agents traced him ; and so wretched is the manner in which the poor and friendless are sepulchred in that vast wealthy city, that when I fain would have had the corpse exhumed, that I might look on the familiar face once more, and convey the remains to some more fitting resting-place, I was told that this was

impossible. Into those festering charnel-houses
where the obscure dead are thrust it is death to enter;
nor could the men who buried the nameless stranger
remember into which grave they had flung his unknown remains. It was only by means of a letter
found upon him that my wretched cousin was traced.
This letter—addressed to Mrs. Adams, of Monk's
Alley—had been preserved by the keeper of the
dead-house where the corpse was carried after the
miserable drunkards' brawl in which your unhappy
father perished. The man who slew him escaped in
the confusion that followed his death. I doubt not
that in such places they favour the escape of a mur-
derer rather than be called to bear witness at his
trial.'

'And the letter, dear madam—did that tell you
much?'

'But little. 'Twas only a few lines of farewell
to the unhappy Amelia. It convinced me, however,
that my cousin had left her with the intention of
never returning. He bequeathed her and his child
to my compassion. Whether he had indeed medi-
tated self-slaughter, as his letter to me hinted, or
whether he intended to seek new fortunes abroad,
when death by an assassin's hand overtook him, I

know not. His ashes rest among the bones of
paupers in St. Anne's churchyard, Soho, in which
parish is the tavern where he fell ; and all that affection could do for his memory was to put up a
tablet in the church, inscribed with his name and
the date of his death.'

'Affection for his memory has done more than
that, dear lady : it has cherished his orphan son.'

'That is but a poor atonement, Robert, from her
whose pride helped to destroy him. If I could have
brought him back to life by the sacrifice of my own,
I would have done it; but I could do nothing for
him, though but two short years before one word of
mine might have saved him. This is what makes
the burden of our sins so heavy—there is no un-
doing them. Pride is a luxury that is apt to cost us
dear, cousin.'

'Did you find a certificate of my mother's marriage amongst my father's papers, madam, which
I presume you examined ? '

'No, Robert. I did indeed ransack an old leathern
portmanteau crammed with papers, and poor ragged
clothing, and tattered books. The papers were for
the most part rough proofs of pamphlets, and odd
pages of manuscript, so scored and blotted as to be

almost illegible. Scattered amongst these were a few tavern-bills, and notes from boon companions, signed but with Christian names or initials, and all bespeaking the wild reckless life of him to whom they were addressed.'

'And there was nothing more ?'

'Nothing. Any more important papers your father had doubtless destroyed, not caring to leave the evidence of his former estate behind him. As he had suppressed his real name, it was natural he should do away with all documents revealing it.'

'I am sorry you can give me no record of my mother's marriage,' I answered sadly.

Lady Barbara was silent, and I knew thereby that she doubted whether any religious ceremonial had ever sanctified the luckless union to which I owed my birth.

I inquired presently where my mother was buried.

'In the graveyard of St. Bride's Church, near which she died,' replied Lady Barbara. 'Her father had been dead six months when I discovered the poor creature; and to have carried her remains to Pennington, where he had lived, would have been only to cause scandal. It was better that the poor soul should rest in the great city, where all private

sorrows and domestic shipwrecks are ingulfed and
hidden beneath the stormy public sea.'

'All that you did was for the wisest, dear madam,'
I replied, kissing the beautiful white hand which
was the bounteous giver of all my earthly blessings.

'And now, dear Robert, I want to act wisely in
planning your future,' my lady said gently. 'I
cannot give you a fortune, but I hope I may help
you to make one. I have concluded that with your
learning the Bar would be your best profession; and
I would have you proceed to London without delay,
and enter yourself at the Temple, where you can
study at your ease under the direction of a respectable
gentleman to whom I can recommend you, and of
whose kindness I have no doubt. I shall give you a
starting sum of two hundred pounds, and will give you
as much every year until your profession shall afford
you a comfortable livelihood, since I wish you to
live like a gentleman, yet with strict economy. I
will not weary you with the hackneyed warnings
against the perils of London life, but I will only bid
you to remember the sad end of your father's reckless
career. If you will not take counsel from that awful
lesson, you will be warned by nothing. But I hope

much from your love of learning, and the natural steadiness of your disposition.'

How could I find words to acknowledge so much goodness! I knelt at my cousin's feet and kissed the dear hands, which I bedewed this time with grateful tears.

'Come, come, Robert, you take these things too seriously,' cried my lady, with affected gaiety. 'Let us talk of your journey. Foolish boy, I am in haste to be rid of you! Shall you be ready to leave us in a week?'

'It is my duty to be ready whenever you please.'

'Ah, Robert, do you think it pleases me to banish you? But Sir Marcus would have no mercy if you came between him and his ambition. Yes, in a week, dear child; it will be best and wisest.'

I was still kneeling at the generous creature's feet. She laid her hand lightly upon my hair, and bent her stately head until her lips touched my forehead; and with a tender motherly kiss she dismissed me.

CHAPTER VIII.

'Twas now late in October, and bleak autumn
winds were fast stripping the park and woods of
summer foliage. For some time past I had seen
but little of Mr. Lestrange, who spent the greater
part of his time out of doors, and left Miss Hemsley
free to follow her own pursuits, and to give as much
of her company as she pleased to Lady Barbara and
myself. She seemed happy with us, after a subdued fashion of her own, but was never beguiled
into gaiety; and I could not refrain from the idea
that her spirits were oppressed by the sense of a
bondage which she had not the courage to shake off.

Mr. Lestrange, for his part, appeared to take
little trouble to secure her good graces. He treated
her sometimes with a free-and-easy politeness,
sometimes with an ill-concealed anger; and bitter
and biting were the speeches which he occasionally

addressed to her. His insults she received with a noble dignity; and nothing could be more cold than her acknowledgment of his compliments.

One day, in a moment of vexation against this dear young lady, the gentleman was so ill-advised as to betray his anger to me.

'She hates me,' he cried savagely, 'and lets me see that she hates me, and knows that I see it. But what of that? she will marry me all the same. My father means it, and I mean it, and when the time comes her whims and caprices will serve her no more than the fluttering of his wings serves a snared bird. Do you think that weak, timid creature would dare set her will against my father's— her legal guardian, and trustee to her fortune—and say no when he says yes? 'Tis all very well to give herself airs and graces with me, but she knows that her fate is as fixed as if she had been bought in the slave-market of Ispahan.'

'That is a hard way to talk of a woman whom you pretend to love,' said I.

'Who says I pretend to love her? I make no pretence: but I mean to marry her. Mark that, Mr. Ainsleigh, and let no puppy-dog who values his ears come between her and me.'

Upon this we came to high words, and might have perhaps proceeded to blows, but were happily interrupted before we arrived at that extremity.

I cannot describe the contempt which I entertained for Everard Lestrange after this revelation of his character. I held myself as much aloof from him as possible, whereupon he affected to treat me with a haughty distance, and took no pains to conceal the fact that he considered me infinitely his inferior.

He had been absent from Hauteville several times during the summer and autumn, having business which compelled him to go to London, as he informed us; though I judged from his father's offended manner on such occasions, that these visits were by no means so necessary as Mr. Lestrange pretended.

He was absent at the time of my confidential conversation with Lady Barbara, and did not return until the next day, when he affected extreme surprise on hearing of my intended departure.

' And are you going to mount a stool in a scrivener's office, or to try your fortune in trade, Master Bob ?' he asked, with a supercilious grin.

' Neither,' I replied ; ' I am going to read for the Bar.'

'Indeed ! with a view to becoming Lord Chancellor,
I suppose ?'

'With a view to doing my best to prove myself
worthy of the kindness I have received,' I answered.

'Heavens ! what a starched prig thou art !' cried
Mr. Lestrange; 'but I'll warrant when once thou hast
thy liberty in London thou wilt waste more time in
taverns, and run after more milliner-girls than the
wildest of us. For a thorough-going rakehell I will
back Tartuffe against Don Juan, with long odds.'

Miss Hemsley also heard of my plans with surprise; and I could not but think that her manner
betrayed despondency. Our Spanish studies were
abandoned.

'It is not worth while going on,' she said; 'a
week is so soon gone, and you must have so many
preparations to make. I fear you will soon forget
your Spanish.'

'Never; nor yet the kind mistress who taught me,'
I answered warmly; and then we both stood silent,
confused, and downcast.

'I hope we shall see you sometimes in town; we
are to spend the winter there, you know,' she said at
last.

'I hope so, dear Miss Hemsley.'

'But surely you will come often to St. James's Square?'

'If Lady Barbara bids me, I shall only be too happy to come.'

'And you—my aunt's cousin—will wait to be bidden? How ceremonious you have grown all at once!'

'Life has pleasant dreams, dear young lady; but sooner or later the hour comes in which the dreamer awakens.'

'What does that mean, Mr. Ainsleigh?' she asked, with a timid, half-conscious smile.

'It means that I have been too happy in this dear place, and that the time has come in which I must bid those I love farewell and begin the battle of life.'

With this I left her, having already said more than I cared to say.

The first half of my last week at Hauteville passed only too quickly. I packed my trunks, which were amply furnished with the clothes supplied by the Warborough tailor, and a box of books, chiefly neat duodecimo volumes of the classics, which Lady Barbara bade me choose from the library.

My good Anthony assisted me to select these, and showed much regret at my approaching departure;

while his sour wife expressed only one sentiment, and that a contemptuous surprise that a learned profession should have been chosen for me.

'I suppose you would rather starve as a fine gentleman than grow rich in a city warehouse,' she said.

'I prefer a profession which befits my parentage, but have no more desire to become a fine gentleman than I have present fear of starvation,' I answered coldly.

'You carry yourself with a high spirit, Mr. Robert; but I have seen prouder spirits than yours brought to the dust.'

As the time for my journey drew near, I bethought me that I must bid good-bye to my old friends of the warrener's lodge, and I blushed as I remembered how small a place those kind, honest creatures had of late occupied in my thoughts; nor had I seen them many times during the last few months, since I had preferred to absent myself altogether from the cottage rather than to go thither accompanied by Mr. Lestrange, whose manner of rallying me on a supposed secret attachment between myself and Margery was to the last degree unpleasant.

When my trunks were packed, and while Everard Lestrange was in London, whither he had gone sud-

denly and in hot haste a day or two before, I walked
down to the dear old cottage where my childhood was
spent. I found my foster-mother alone at her spin-
ning-wheel, from which she rose to greet me. One
glance at the familiar face showed me that its natural
cheerfulness was exchanged for an anxious gravity,
which at once puzzled and alarmed me.

'Oh, Robin, what a stranger thou art!' she cried,
as we shook hands.

'And even now I have but come to bid you good
bye, dear mother.'

The good soul was grieved to lose me, little as I
had of late done to prove myself worthy her
affection. She talked, however, of the wonderful
change of fortune that had befallen me, and rejoiced
in my altered prospects, even though good fortune
was to carry me away from old friends.

'I shall always remember thee a babe in my arms,
Robin,' she said tenderly. 'I may call thee Robin
still, may I not? though they tell me thou art
called Mr. Ainsleigh at the great house. Jack and
I always suspected as much.'

'Suspected what, mother?'

'That thou wert Roderick Ainsleigh's son. Why,
thou hadst his very face from a baby; and others

suspected the same, or knew it, maybe. That is why Martha Grimshaw has always hated thee.'

'Why should she hate me for being Roderick Ainsleigh's son?'

'Because she loved Roderick Ainsleigh. Yes, Robin, I was house-maid at Hauteville Hall in those days, and servants sometimes know more than their betters. Martha Peyton was mad for love of Mr. Ainsleigh, and was fool enough to fancy he loved her. I'll not say that he did not make her a fine speech now and then, or steal a kiss when he chanced to meet her in the corridor, but 'twas no more than such court as any fine gentleman may pay to his sweetheart's waiting-maid; and Roderick Ainsleigh had neither good nor evil thoughts about Martha, who was no beauty at the best of times. But she took it all seriously, and was always hanging about wherever her lady's cousin was to be met, and would run a mile to open a door for him; and when his marriage with Lady Barbara was talked of in the servants' hall Martha would laugh and say nobody would ever dance at that wedding. But one day she said something to Mr. Ainsleigh that let him know she thought he was paying serious court to her, and he burst out laughing, and told her the

truth,—that he had given her kisses and compliments and guineas because he wanted her good word
with her mistress.   I came upon him in the corridor
as he was saying this, and saw Martha's face.
'Twas black as thunder. She stood fixed like a
statue on the spot where he left her, staring like one
that was struck blind or foolish, and after this time
I never saw her speak to Mr. Ainsleigh.   If she met
him she dropped him a low curtsey, and passed on.
And I think from this time she began to plot mischief against him.   When she found she couldn't
have him herself, she was determined nobody else
should have him.'

'Why didn't you warn Lady Barbara?'

'I warn her? Do you think she would have
suffered me to talk of her business? and could I
turn informer against a fellow-servant? You don't
know what the servants' hall is. Besides, I didn't
think Martha could do much mischief, though I
knew it was in her heart to try it. 'Twas only when
Mr. Ainsleigh went away that I knew there was real
harm done. Ah, Robin, 'tis a hard world we live
in, and full of trouble!'

She gave a heavy sigh, and I saw her eyes fill
with tears.

'Yes, dear mother, for some of us; but God forbid trouble should come to you.'

'It has come, Robin,' she answered, gazing at me with an eager, scrutinizing look that I had never seen in her face before. 'I have but one child, and to see her sad is the worst of sadness to me.'

'Margery sad?' cried I; 'when last I saw her she was as gay as a woodland fairy.'

'When last you saw her? Do you see her so seldom, Robin?'

'Except at church, I have not seen her for weeks. You must not take it unkind that I have stopped away; I have had good reasons.'

'Ay, Robin, good reasons I doubt not. But have you never met Madge by chance in the woods all this time? She spends much of her time in the woods. 'Tis hard to keep her indoors in fine weather, and she is not so easily managed as she once was. Oh, Robin, my child is wretched, and I cannot find out the cause; and 'tis breaking this poor heart!'

And here the good creature burst into tears. I tried to comfort her, but her tears flowed only the faster.

'She is wretched, Robin, and will not tell her

mother the cause of her grief. Oh! if thou didst not love her, why didst thou beguile and deceive her with fine words and promises?'

'I beguile! I deceive! Mother, as God is my judge, I have never spoken to Margery but as a brother should speak to his sister. I have never loved her with more or less than a brother's affection, and I would not let the man live that should deceive or wrong her.'

'Ah, Robin, thou speakest fair, but I know the child loves thee. Her father and I have joked her about thee many a time, pleased to see her blushes and smiles. We did not think thou couldst fail to love her, and we did not know they would acknowledge thee for Roderick Ainsleigh's son, and make a fine gentleman of thee. Yes, Robin, she loved thee better than a sister loves a brother, and I thought she was loved in return; others said as much.'

'What others?'

'Martha Grimshaw and Mr. Lestrange. He told me thou wert mad for her.'

'He told a lie. Those two are my enemies both, and would be glad to do me a mischief. But, mother, I do love my little foster-sister, and if it

will ease your mind to see her my wife I will marry
her when you will.   She is the loveliest creature I
ever saw, and might turn the heads of wiser men;
but 'twas my fate not long ago to see a face that
bewitched me, and to give my love where it can
never be returned.   Shall I waste my life in weeping
for a shadow ?   No, dear mother; give me Margery
for a wife, and I will work for her honestly, and be
as true a husband as ever woman had.'

'Nay, Robin, I will not beg a husband for my
daughter.   Thou dost not love her as we thought
thou didst.   'Tis ourselves we must blame for
judging amiss.   All I know is that the child has
some trouble on her mind, and I thought thou
might'st be at the bottom of it.'

Again she scrutinized my face with anxious looks,
and then turned away, shaking her head sorrow-
fully.

'There is something amiss,' she said, 'but I
know not what.'

'You spoke just now of Mr. Lestrange,' said I.
'Has he been hanging about this place of late ?'

'No, Robin; I'll have no fine London gentleman about my place.   He came two or three times
without you, but I gave him sour looks that told

him he wasn't wanted; and the last time he was here, full two months ago, he told me he was going to London for the rest of the year.'

' And since then you have seen him no more ? '

' No.'

' Yet he has not been all the time in town. He has run backwards and forwards, but has spent most of the time at Hauteville.'

I remembered his broadly-declared admiration of the rustic beauty ; I considered his hideous code of morals, and trembled for my innocent foster-sister.

'God defend her from such a libertine!' I thought, and blamed the selfishness that had kept me so long away from the warrener's lodge.

I would fain have seen and talked to Margery before leaving Berkshire, and so waited for some hours in the hope that she would return, but she did not come. Jack Hawker came home to his supper, but his manner was cold and sullen, and I perceived that some dark suspicion had turned the hearts of these two friends against me. I left the cottage at last, disheartened and uneasy, and re-turned to Hauteville, there to spend a somewhat melancholy evening with my patroness and Miss Hemsley.

The next day returned Mr. Lestrange, and soon after Sir Marcus, who had been on a visit to a nobleman's seat in the adjoining county. I spent the morning *tête-à-tête* with Anthony Grimshaw, while Lady Barbara and Miss Hemsley drove to the nearest town to pay visits and make purchases. It seemed sad to me to lose their company on this, almost the last day of my residence at Hauteville; but I felt it was a fortunate accident which divided me from Dorothea Hemsley. In her presence I found it hard to fetter my tongue, and Lady Barbara's reproachful looks often reminded me of my imprudence. Soon, too soon, was I to be separated from her for ever; for I felt that, once away from Hauteville, I should be as remote from her as if we had been inhabitants of different planets.

The day wore on ; we dined in stately solemnity ; and I was pacing the terrace alone, awaiting a summons to take tea with the two ladies in the long drawing-room, when I was accosted by a footman, who came to inform me that Sir Marcus Lestrange wished to speak with me in his study. It was the first time he had ever sent for me ; but I concluded that he was about to offer me some parting advice, or to favour me with a valedictory address. I therefore obeyed without any sentiment of uneasiness, regretting only that if the diplomatist should prove tedious, I might lose my privileged half-hour with the ladies.

The study in which Sir Marcus spent so many hours of his life was a dark and somewhat gloomy oak-panelled apartment, furnished with bookcases containing ponderous folios, and with numerous oaken chests and iron cases, which I supposed to contain papers. A carved-oak desk occupied the centre of the room, and on this, though it was not yet quite dark, some half-dozen candles were burning in a brazen candelabrum.

My patron was not alone; a solemn assembly had been convoked in haste, and I found myself placed before these as a prisoner at the bar of justice. Lady Barbara sat opposite her husband, pale as death; Miss Hemsley close beside her, with an anxious, distressed countenance. Next to his father stood Mr. Lestrange, and I thought he greeted me with a glance of triumph as I entered the room. At a respectful distance from the rest appeared Mrs. Grimshaw, and I knew her presence boded ill to me.

'Mr. Ainsleigh,' began Sir Marcus, in a severe

magisterial voice, 'you have been rescued from abject poverty; you have been received into this house and liberally entertained for the last ten years of your life; you have enjoyed the education of a gentleman, and, finally, you have been admitted into the bosom of this family on a footing of equality, much to my regret, and all by the charity of Lady Barbara Lestrange yonder.'

'No, Marcus,' said my lady, 'I will not have it called charity.'

'By what other name would your ladyship call it? What claim, legal or social, had your cousin's bastard upon you?'

At sound of that bitter epithet, my lady winced as if she had been struck. 'It ill becomes you to call him by so cruel a name,' she said; 'we have no knowledge that his mother was not lawfully wedded to my cousin Roderick.'

'Have we any proof that she was? Mr. Ainsleigh's reputation is against the probability that he would make an honest woman of a parson's runaway daughter, who left her home to follow him.'

'I cannot stay here, sir, to hear my mother belied.'

'You will stay here, sir, as long as I please.'

'Not to hear you speak ill of the dead; that I will not suffer. I am fully conscious of the benefits I owe to Lady Barbara, and thank her for them with all my heart, and in my prayers morning and night; but I know not why I am called hither to be reminded of my obligations, or what I have done to deserve that they should be cast in my face with so much harshness.'

'You know not what you have done!' cried Sir Marcus. 'I suppose you are impudent enough to pretend not to know that John Hawker's daughter has left her home secretly, as your mother left hers?'

'Indeed, I know nothing of the kind, nor do I believe that it is so. I was at the warrener's lodge yesterday afternoon, and heard nothing of this.'

'And the girl ran away last night. Oh, no doubt you laid your plans wisely, and now you act astonishment as naturally as Garrick himself. But Hawker is in the steward's room; you will look otherwise when you see him.'

Here Miss Hemsley would fain have left the apartment, but Sir Marcus forbade her.

'Indeed, sir, I have nothing to do with this,' she said; 'I beg to be allowed to retire.'

'No, Dorothea, I must bid you stay. This gentle-man has been a favourite of yours, I hear; it is well that you should discover his real character.'

'O sir, you are very cruel,' the girl murmured tearfully.

'If Margery Hawker has left her home, Sir Marcus,' I said, 'there is no one will regret it more than I; and there is no one less concerned in her leaving.'

'What! you will swear to that, I suppose?'

'With my dying breath, if needs be. Yes, at the very moment when my soul goes forth to meet its God.'

'I believe him,' cried Lady Barbara. 'It is not in my cousin's blood to tell a lie.'

'You will have cause to change your opinion presently, madam,' replied her husband coldly; and then, turning to me, he went on, 'you are a per-jurer and a blasphemer, sir, and your own hand is the witness against you. Have you ever seen that before?'

He handed me an open letter, written in a hand so like my own, and with a signature so adroitly counterfeited that I stood aghast, with the paper in my hand, staring at it in utter bewilderment.

'Come, sir, the play has lasted long enough, and

'tis time you answered my question. I think you'll scarce deny your knowledge of that handwriting.'

' I know the handwriting well enough, Sir Marcus, for it is the most ingenious forgery that ever was executed; but I never looked upon this paper before.'

' Great Heaven, was there ever such an impudent denial! And you protest that you never saw that letter till this moment?'

'Never, sir.'

' Perhaps you will be so good as to read it aloud for the benefit of the company, especially for Lady Barbara, who believes in your innocence?'

' I am quite willing Lady Barbara should hear this vile forgery, sir,' I replied, and then read the letter, which ran thus:—

' DEAREST MARGERY,—For fear there should at last be some mistake about the coach, I write in haste to bid you remember that it leaves the " George " at Warborough at nine o'clock at night. Your place is taken, and you have nothing to do but alight at the " Bull and Mouth " in the City, where you will ask for Mrs. Jones, who will meet you there without fail. She is a good motherly soul, and will take care of you till you are joined by one who loves you better than life, which will be in three days at latest. And then, beloved girl, far from those new grand friends who would divide us, I will teach thee how faithfully this heart, which has long languished in secret, can love the fairest and dearest of women.—Ever and ever thy fond lover,

'ROBERT AINSLEIGH.'

'What think you now, Lady Barbara?' asked Sir Marcus.

'As I have a soul to be saved, madam,' cried I, 'no word of that vile letter ever was penned by this hand!'

'There are some folks to whom a false oath comes easy, sir,' said the baronet. 'You did not think that letter would fall into my hands; it was intended for your victim, who would have cherished the precious paper, hidden against her heart, I dare swear. Unluckily for you, the post played you false, and the letter was delivered this morning, twelve hours after the bird had flown. The wretched broken-hearted father of this weak and wicked girl brought it down to me, and calls upon me to punish the traitor who has ruined his child.'

'That, sir, I trust you will do, if Providence helps

me to find him,' I answered, looking straight at Mr. Lestrange, who received my gaze without flinching. Was he not, by his own account, steeped to the lips in vice, and past-master in the art of dissimulation ? ' But as for that letter,' I continued, ' I again protest, and for the last time, that it is a forgery.'

' And pray, sir, is there any one so much interested in your insignificant fortunes as to take the trouble to counterfeit your handwriting ? '

' It is always the interest of an enemy to work mischief, sir; and there are few creatures so insignificant as to escape all enmity. Again, sir, self-interest may have prompted the forging of that letter. The traitor who is really concerned in the flight of this dear girl would best escape the consequences of his crime by shifting it upon the shoulders of an innocent person.'

'I have not condemned you hastily, sir,' said Sir Marcus. 'Here is a sheet of Spanish exercises in your hand, with your signature scribbled at the bottom of the page. I have carefully compared the letter with this paper, and I find the signatures agree to the most minute curve.'

'Conclusive evidence that the letter is a forgery, sir,' I replied boldly. 'Experts in handwriting have agreed that no man ever signs his name twice alike; there is always some minute difference. A will was once pronounced a forgery upon that very ground — the several signatures at the bottom of the several pages were all precisely alike.'

'I see, sir, you have already learned to advance precedents and argue like a lawyer. Perhaps you will be less eloquent when confronted with the father of your victim.'

Sir Marcus rang a bell, and ordered the servant who answered it to send in John Hawker. There was a dead silence while we waited his coming. I heard the slow, shambling step of my foster-father on the stone floor of the passage, and my heart bled for him in his trouble.

He came slowly into the room, and stood amongst us, with his bare head bent by the first shame that had ever bowed it.

'Your foster-son denies that he wrote the letter which you brought me this morning, Hawker,' said Sir Marcus, in his hard magisterial voice.

'I know naught of that, sir; I can't read writing myself. I took the letter to the parson at Pennington, and he read it to me; and when he came to the name at the bottom, I'd as lieve he'd put a knife through my heart as have read that name to me.'

'It is clear that some person has tempted your daughter away. Is there any one except Robert Ainsleigh whom you could suppose concerned in her flight?'

'Nay, sir, the poor child had no acquaintance except Robin yonder, and your son.'

'My son! Do you pretend to rank my son amongst your daughter's acquaintance?'

''Tis likely enough he'll do so,' cried Mr. Lestrange, with a contemptuous laugh; 'Ainsleigh took me to his cottage once or twice to get some artificial flies for our trout-fishing.'

'Ay, sir, and you came many times afterward without Robin, and won all our hearts by your pleasant familiar ways, till my wife bethought herself 'twas a dangerous thing to have a fine gentleman hanging about the place, and let you see that you wasn't welcome any longer.'

'Why, fellow, it is three months since I crossed your threshold.'

'And if you had crossed it but yesterday, Everard, I do not suppose this man would dare accuse my son,' exclaimed Sir Marcus indignantly; 'and that in the face of a letter which proclaims the real delinquent.'

'I accuse no one, sir,' replied Jack Hawker; 'I only know that my child has left me and her mother, and broken two loving hearts.'

On this I turned to my foster-father.

'John Hawker,' said I, 'you yourself have had as much hand in this miserable business as I have. I have ever regarded your daughter as my dear foster-sister, and my conduct to her has always been that of a brother. I told your wife as much yesterday, before this trouble arose; I tell you so to-day. But if you can find her, and bring her to me, an honest woman, I will make her my wife, and cherish and honour her as such so long as I live; though I will hide from no one here that I have bestowed my heart elsewhere, where I have no hope that it can ever be accepted, and can never give her a lover's passionate affection.'

'I protest that is an honest man's offer,' cried Lady Barbara.

'Ay,' sneered her husband, 'your hopeful *protégé* promises to marry the girl if her father can find her; rely on it, your honest man will take care she is not found; that good motherly soul, Mrs. Jones, will know how to guard her charge.—And now, sir,' he continued, addressing himself to me, ' understand that you are found out, and stand convicted under your own handwriting, and that no cry of forgery will serve you, however impudently persisted in. You will therefore oblige me by quitting this house to-night at your earliest convenience, and you will further comprehend that Lady Barbara washes her hands of you, and that any communication which you may hereafter take the trouble to address to her will be returned to you with the seal unbroken.'

' Honoured madam, my dear kinswoman, does this gentleman speak your will?' I asked, looking straight at my benefactress.

'There are circumstances, Robert, in which a woman's will must needs be that of her husband,' Lady Barbara replied.

'In that case, dear madam, I submit. No unconscious wrong which you may do me in the present can cancel my debt of gratitude for the past. I was doomed to leave this dear place. That I leave in unmerited disgrace can add but one more pang to the anguish of parting.'

I bowed low to my lady and to Miss Hemsley,

and turned to quit the room; but before going I approached my foster-father.

'Jack,' I said, offering him my hand, 'you cannot think me so base a wretch as this vile counterfeit letter would make me? Shake hands, and bid me God speed; and if it is possible for a man that's ignorant of the town, I'll find your daughter.'

'Ah, Robin, thou know'st but too well where to find her. 'Tis thy name that's wrote at bottom of the letter. The parson said so, and he'd not tell a lie. I'll never shake thy hand again, Robin, for thou'rt a villain!'

This stung me more sharply than the abuse of Sir Marcus. I left the room hurriedly, ran to my own chamber, and packed a portmanteau in haste with my immediate necessaries. The rest of my luggage was ready packed; but this I left to be sent after me, leaving it to Lady Barbara's pleasure whether I had the things or not.

With the small portmanteau in my hand, I ran downstairs. It was now dark; the lamps were not yet lit, and the graat hall was but dimly lighted by a wood-fire. I was leaving the house, when a door in the hall was softly opened, and I heard my name whispered.

It was Lady Barbara who called me. She was standing just within the door of a small waiting-room near the grand entrance, ordinarily used by footmen and humble visitors. She took my hands in hers and drew me hastily into the room, which was lighted by one wax taper. Even in that dim light I could see she had been weeping.

'Dear child,' she cried, 'it is hard to part with you thus; but our enemies are too strong for us, and we must submit. My little child lies in the cemetery at Madrid, and I am not allowed to cherish my cousin's orphan son.'

'Oh! dear madam, you do not think me guilty? Say but that, and I am happy.'

'I say it with all my heart, Robert. The letter is a forgery, and it is all a base plot against you, because I am mistress of my own fortune, and might bequeath it to you. What do I say? My husband is incapable of such infamy; but there are those who would hesitate at no villany that would bring them wealth and power. You are my adopted son, Robert; remember that. Nothing can sever that tie between us—no, not even ill-conduct or ingratitude of yours—for I am more charitable now than I was when my pride slew your father. Do not answer me, I have but a few stolen moments to give you.   Take this note-book; it contains all the ready-money I can command to-night, and there is a letter in it, a few hurried lines of recommendation, which you will carry to Mr. Swinfen, of Paper Buildings.   You will go straight to London, and you must write and tell me how things prosper with you.   Write to me under cover to Mrs. Winbolt, at 49 Long Acre—she is my milliner, and a good soul. And now, good-bye.   Stay, I am to give you this from Dora : it is a book she has used for the last five years.'

It was a shabby duodecimo volume, which I put in my breast, too much moved for words.   If it had been some jewelled box containing the relics of St. Peter, it could scarce have exercised a more healing influence upon the sore heart that beat against it.

'God bless her and you, dear cousin, and fare-well!' and with this I wrung my kinswoman's hand, and left her.

The autumn night was chill and bleak, and the full moon rode high above the sombre leafless woods as I left Hauteville.   The little book in my bosom— a Spanish translation of the *Imitation of Christ*— and the memory of Lady Barbara's goodness were the only consolers that I carried with me into the world of which I knew no more than an infant. Once, and once only, did I look back at the old Elizabethan mansion, with lighted windows glowing in the distance. O God, how long before I was again to look upon those walls! What perils by land and perils by sea, what agonies of hope deferred and dull despair, was I to suffer before I revisited that familiar spot!

CHAPTER IX.

I GO TO LONDON.

IT was at the George Inn, Warborough, that I spent the wretched night of my departure from Hauteville; but not in sleep. Slow and dreary were the hours, as I lay in a small room of the inn, thinking of all I had lost, and the utter loneliness of the life that lay before me. I had opened and kissed Miss Hemsley's little Spanish volume, and had striven to pin my mind to those pious sentences of Kempis, or Gersen, or whoever else was the saintly creature who had composed them. But my spirit was too wide of that calm mystic region which the recluse inhabited, and I could not yet bring myself to take comfort from a consoler whose experience had so little in common with my own sorrows. I could but lay the precious volume under my pillow, as a charm or talisman, and then lie broad awake thinking of my hard fate, which had from my very cradle—nay, before my birth itself—made me a mark for the poisoned arrows of hate.

I had not even so much curiosity as to open the note-book thrust upon me by my generous mistress. What cared I how rich or how poor I was to enter on my strange, friendless life? It was enough for me to know that my dear benefactress still loved and trusted me; and this knowledge was more precious to me than all the wealth of the Great Mogul, of whom I had lately read in the Jesuit Bernier's travels.

Before leaving Warborough I made all possible inquiries about the missing girl for whose absence I had been so unjustly blamed. After much questioning, and going from one person to another, I found one of the hangers-on of the coach-yard, who remembered to have seen Jack Hawker's daughter leave by the night mail, so close-hooded that it was only by accident he had caught a glimpse of her face, which he remembered by having seen her at market with her mother. He wondered what should be taking the girl to London, and made bold to ask her whether she was going out to service; but she had answered only by a shake of her head.

On this I went to the coach-office and questioned

the clerk who booked the passengers' places; but here I could discover nothing to cast light upon Margery's departure. The places had all been engaged by persons of the male sex, but the clerk remembered one of these persons saying that the single place he engaged was wanted for a young woman. I sought in vain to obtain a description of this man. The clerk could only tell me that he looked like a gentleman's servant.

'I suppose you know all the servants at Hauteville Hall by sight?' I said; but the young man replied in the negative.

'Was the man who took the place short and stout, with reddish hair?' I asked.

'I rather think it was some such person,' replied the clerk; 'but as I didn't observe him closely I would scarce venture to be positive. He seemed in amazing haste to be gone.'

The person I described was Mr. Lestrange's valet and confidential follower; for I could not but think that gentleman was at the bottom of my foster-sister's flight, and had forged—or ordered the forging of—the letter which flung the guilt on me. I had good cause to know him as an unprincipled profligate, by the witness of his own lips; and I had heard his broadly-declared admiration of Margery. Nor could I forget the malignant look which he had given me when he surprised me on my knees at Miss Hemsley's feet. To gratify his own wickedness, and at the same time to ruin me in the estimation of my Hauteville friends, would be a double stroke of mischief to delight that cruel and treacherous nature.

I arrived in London at dusk, and great was my wonder at the vastness of the city; the gaudy, painted signs of merchants and chapmen swinging across the street; the sedan-chairs with running footmen carrying flambeaux, which we met at the court-end of the town; the pitch-blackened heads of the Scottish rebels rotting on Temple Bar; the roar and turmoil; the noisy hucksters and impudent beggars who assailed the coach-door; the newsboys bellowing and blowing horns with as much excitement as if the Pretender had again landed on our shores, or the king been stabbed in his coach by some Jacobite desperado. At any other time I should doubtless have been both amused and delighted by the strangeness of these things; but my heart was burdened with too many cares and troubles, and I looked upon all I saw as on the scenes that pass before one's eyes in a dream—mere confused pictures in which one has no part.

It was, of course, too late to deliver my letter of recommendation to Mr. Swinfen, so I lay at the inn where the coach stopped, and spent another sleepless night in a stifling chamber, the one small window whereof opened upon a covered gallery that ran round the inner quadrangle of the house. The strange noises, the brawling of some drunken revellers in an apartment below, the arrival of ponderous waggons and coaches which lumbered into the court-yard long before cock-crow, would have deprived me of slumber even if my own uneasy thoughts had not been sufficient to keep me awake; and at cock-crow began shrill cries and bawlings of hucksters in the street without, mingled with a constant rumbling of wheels.

Never, I think, had I known the meaning of the word solitude until that bitter morning, when I seated myself in a darksome little den, or partitioned corner of the coffee-room, called a box, and breakfasted alone in London. Crusoe on his desert island had at least the animal creation wherewith to consort; but I, in all this vast metropolis, knew not

so much as a dog. Nor did the friendly looks of
strangers invite my confidence. Roughness and im-
politeness marked the manners of all I had hitherto
encountered. Even the waiters seemed to regard
me with suspicious looks; and I doubt not that my
gloomy face and dispirited manner were calculated
to inspire curiosity and disgust. The man who
cannot face the world with a smile is likely to be
suspected of having some sinister cause for his
despondency. I breakfasted quickly, and it was but
eight o'clock when I had finished—too early an
hour, most certainly, for a ceremonial visit to Mr.
Swinfen. Nor had I the smallest inclination to
explore the town, of whose wonders I had heard so
much. What are sights and wonders to the man
who has just been abruptly torn from all he loves?
St. Peter's at Rome may be at his elbow, and he
will scarce raise his weary eyes to look at it. The
shadow of Pisa's leaning tower may slope across his
pathway, and he will hardly take the trouble to
glance from the shadow to the substance. I sat
listlessly, with my arms folded on the little table
before me, listening idly to the talk of customers
ordering breakfast, and waiters attending upon
them.

I had sat thus for nearly an hour, when I bethought myself of Lady Barbara's note-book, and, to while away the time, set myself to examine its contents. It was a memorandum-book, originally of some twenty pages, but all except three of these had been torn out. One silken pocket was crammed with bank-notes, which I unfolded, and found to amount to near three hundred pounds. But in another pocket there was something more precious than these bills on the directors of the Bank of England. This was an oval crystal locket, with gold rim, containing a miniature likeness of my dear lady, and a lock of dark hair, which I knew for hers. Nor was this all the comfort hidden in the tiny volume. One of the pages was inscribed with sentences of hope and counsel in Latin and English, hastily written for my consolation by the hand of my dear benefactress :—

'*Sperate, et vosmet rebus servate secundis.*

The Lord also will be a refuge for the oppressed, a refuge in times of trouble.

Commit thy way unto the Lord. . . . Rest in the Lord and wait patiently for Him.

The wicked plotteth against the just.

The steps of a good man are ordered by the Lord: and he delighteth in His way.

Though he fall he shall not be utterly cast down : for the Lord upholdeth him with His hand.

Tu fortis sis animo, et tua moderatio, constantia, eorum infamet injuriam.'

I was thus rich in money and in friendship; and I began to feel that to persist in a dull and obstinate despair when so much yet remained to me would be beyond measure sinful. How different must have been my feelings if Lady Barbara and Dora Hemsley had believed in my guilt! as they might reasonably have done, considering the ingenious evidence that had been contrived against me. Revolving this in my mind, I resolved to face my position boldly, supported by the hope that my own actions might be made to prove the falsehood of my enemies. 'I have my future all before me,' I thought; 'and am my own master. Hitherto I have been a child in leading-strings; my manhood dates from to-day, and it shall be my study so to plan my life that treachery itself cannot assail it. I am not of so proud a nature as my father, and I freely

accept this money from the hands of the dear lady
to whom, under Providence, I owe my very life;
nor is there any painfulness in the knowledge that
I am so much indebted to her. I have youth,
strength, and an excellent education; and it must
go hard with me if with these weapons and a resolute fortitude I do not conquer in the battle of life.
But I have first to learn something of the battle-
ground, of which at present I know no more than
a baby.'

I called for a newspaper, hoping therefrom to
learn something of what was stirring in this busy
city, to which I was so utter a stranger; but the
Daily Courant—a sheet which the waiter brought
me—gave little information on this head. It was
chiefly taken up by our foreign politics, the enor-
mous subsidies or gifts granted to the Empress
Queen and certain German princes; by which it
appeared that Britain had been made to pay very
dearly for a peace that was worse wanted by her
allies than by herself. One paragraph that attracted
my attention was an account of a new colony that
had just been formed in Nova Scotia. Four thousand persons, with their families, had lately em-
barked for this wild, unknown region, tempted by

the liberality of the Government, which offered a free passage out, and a freehold of fifty acres to each settler, with ten years' exemption from all taxes.

'Why should I not go thither,' I thought, 'and flee like a new Æneas from the ashes of my Troy? In that new world, if I had no friends, I should have at least no enemies, and I might make myself a name and a home amongst settlers as friendless as myself.'

The thought was but for a moment. What would home or friends, or name be to me without Dorothea Hemsley.

'Perish the thought of new lands across the sea,' I said to myself; 'I will stay in England and be near the dear girl I love, perhaps to serve her in some hour when she may need the strong arm of a faithful friend.'

To this bold outburst followed sudden despondency. Alas, poor wretch! should I be any nearer Dora at London than at Nova Scotia? She was severed from me by a gulf more impassable than that sea which the American emigrants had traversed under command of Colonel Cornwallis.

At noon I left the inn, and inquired my way to

the Temple. Being now in a somewhat more hopeful frame of mind, I regarded the bustle of the streets with curiosity, and was even amused by the strangeness of all I saw. My way took me again near the gloomy arch which I had ridden under in the coach, and I looked up with a shudder towards those ghastly severed heads which were impaled there as bloody memorials of a nation's severity. I could but think this dreadful exhibition eminently calculated to keep alive the Jacobite feeling which Lady Barbara had told me was by no means drowned in the blood that had been shed since '45, and I wondered much at the foolish policy which had elevated traitors into martyrs.

I was much pleased with the tranquil and studious air of the Temple, whose shadowy courts and solemn squares seemed to me to bespeak it a retreat for learning. I had yet to discover how such appearances may deceive, and how many a shallow pate drinks and games away existence in a suite of chambers, the very atmosphere of which whispers of a Bacon or a Selden.

Mr. Swinfen's apartments I discovered in a handsome row of houses commanding a view of the river, on which I saw innumerable boats plying, and all

the pleasant water-traffic I had read of in the
Spectator. Towering grandly above all meaner
roofs I saw the noble dome of St. Paul's, and beyond
many spires and steeples dimly blue in the hazy
distance, for there was a notable difference between
the sky that overarched this city, and the clear ether
above Hauteville Woods.

The gentleman to whom I was recommended was
happily at home, and received me with much gracious-
ness.

'I would do a great deal to serve any relative of
Lady Barbara's,' he said courteously, after he had
read my patroness's letter; 'I knew her father, and I
remember her ladyship before she married Lestrange.
She spent but one short season in London before
her marriage, and would have been one of the reign-
ing belles of that season but that she was too modest
to appear much in public. And so you are an
Ainsleigh? Are you nearly related to that Roderick
Ainsleigh of whom Lord Hauteville was so fond?'

'I am his only child, sir.'

'Indeed! I did not know he lived so long as to
marry.'

I felt my face flush at this.

'His marriage was an obscure one, sir, and he

died in poverty. But for Lady Barbara's goodness I doubt if I should be living to tell as much. I owe everything to her.'

'And I am glad to see that you are proud to acknowledge your indebtedness,' replied Mr. Swinfen kindly.

After this he talked much to me, examining me as to my education, and directing me in the course which I should have to take in order to prepare for entering the profession which had been chosen for me. I will not linger over the details of this period of my life, since the labour I devoted to the study of the law was wasted work. The career which I thus began was destined to have neither middle nor end, but to be abruptly cut short almost at the outset. Fate called me to a harder life than that of a law-student, and it was my lot to play my humble part in a more stirring drama than was ever enacted in that grave sanctuary of legal lore in which I now took up my abode.

My patron kindly sent one of his clerks with me to hunt for a set of chambers suited to my purse and position.

'You cannot practise too much economy at the outset of your career,' said Mr. Swinfen, just before he dismissed me. 'Advancement at the Bar is a plant of slow growth, and the man is lucky who, after some éight or ten years' patient industry, can command bread and cheese, and wear a decent coat. But if the struggle be a hard one, the prizes are splendid; and the man of parts who can dine on a red herring and a dish of tea, or a fourpenny plate of beef from the eating-house, may hope to mount the woolsack. I trust you have an inward conviction that you are destined to be Lord Chancellor, Mr. Ainsleigh?'

'Indeed no, sir,' I answered, smiling.

'Then I am sorry for it. Every man who passes the Temple gate should say to himself, " Bacon, or nothing!"'

'And suppose it is nothing, sir?'

'For such a man there is no possibility of utter failure. In trying for the highest rung of the ladder he will at least contrive to scramble to the middle. But for the fellow who enters his name at the Temple because it is a genteel thing to do, who spends his nights at Vauxhall, and wastes his substance at cards and in cock-pits, and brings loose-lived women to his chambers, and cheats his tailor to sport a suit of cut velvet in the Ring, the road he

travels is the highway that leads to the dogs. I hope
you are not come to London to be a man of pleasure,
Mr. Ainsleigh ? '

'I have little inclination for pleasure, sir, and not
a single acquaintance in this city.'

' So much the better,' growled Mr. Swinfen ; ' and
now go along with you, for I have half a dozen attor-
ney fellows waiting in the next room.   My clerk will
find you decent chambers, and. will see you safely
through the formalities of your entrance.   Good-day.
Dine with me on Tuesday next, at four o'clock, at
my house in Queen Anne Street.   I have a haunch
from a ducal demesne which will be in prime order
by that time, and you will meet some gentlemen
from whom a nod in public is a patent of social
standing for a youngster.'

I thanked Mr. Swinfen for his kindness, and departed in company of the clerk, a decent elderly
person, who quickly found for me a couple of small
rooms in a house in Brick Court, which was afterwards destined to become famous as the abode of
genius and poetry.   The rooms were at the top of
the house, and commanded an extensive view of roofs
and chimney-pots ; but they were cheap, and of this
advantage I was fully conscious, as I was bent on

extreme economy in my management of Lady Barbara's handsome gift.

When all preliminary ceremonies had been duly gone through, at an outlay which absorbed a good deal of my dear benefactress's money, Mr. Swinfen's clerk left me, and as I stood alone in my somewhat cheerless garret, I felt that now I had begun the world in real earnest.

I sent to the city inn for my portmanteau, and went out myself to purchase certain books which Mr. Swinfen had informed me were necessary for me to possess, at the same time that he offered me free use of his own noble library of law-books, which he bade me to convey to and fro from his chambers to my own, as I needed them.

On the following Tuesday I dined at my patron's house, amongst a party of gentlemen, the youngest of whom was at least twenty years my senior. The talk was of politics and of legal matters. I heard much of the Duke of Newcastle and his brother, Mr. Pelham, and of that rising politician, Mr. Pitt, then only paymaster of the forces, but already exercising considerable influence in the senate. There was also much discussion of the great will case of Barnsley *versus* Powell and others, that had been decided in the previous year, and the details of which had lately been published by a bookseller in Fleet Street. To this and all other conversation I listened with respectful interest, pleased to hear the discourse of clever members of that profession in which it was my earnest desire to prosper.

And now began for me a life of the extremest loneliness. Secluded day after day in my garret-chambers —waited on at rare intervals by a deaf old woman, who came and went with a stolid mechanical air, and looked at me with a dull unseeing gaze as she flourished her well-worn broom or knelt to light my fire, as if scarce conscious of my existence—I was little less remote from the world than if I had been the pious inmate of some cave hewn in the solid rock by one of Iona's early bishops.

On the days when I dined in hall I did certainly exchange some civil commonplaces with my companions at table, but these were would-be beaux, who knew the town, and boasted loudly of their acquaintance with fine gentlemen and their conquests among fine ladies. I was indeed at once horrified and disgusted by the tone in which these scoundrels talked of women of quality, whom I have since discovered they knew only by name. Sometimes towards evening

I found my spirits oppressed by an almost painful
sense of solitude. I felt a desire to hear my own
voice, nay, sometimes even a panic-stricken notion
that I had lost the faculty of speech, so strange
sounded the syllables when I tried to roll out a few
lines of Demosthenes, or demanded with Cicero how
it came to pass that, for the last twenty years, no
man had been my enemy who had not also shown
himself a foe to the republic.

On these occasions, when my eyes ached with long
hours of reading, and my head was heavy from the
continuance of study, I snatched up my hat, ran
downstairs, and went out in the fog and drizzling
rain, or in the bleak winter wind, to loiter in the
crowded streets, and amuse myself with the busy life
about me. And in this the hermit of London has a
supreme advantage over the rustic solitary. Friendless he may be, but never quite companionless, for
in every coffee-house or city tavern he can find company which, if not select, is by no means unin-
structive. While my legal education progressed
steadily in the solitude of my garret-chamber, the
streets and the humbler class of coffee-houses enlightened me as to the ways of the world. I learned
to talk politics, became vastly familiar with the affairs

of the Prince of Wales and his party, railed against the old king for his devotion to ugly women, reviled the Duke of Cumberland, growled at the money taken from us by the Prince of Wolfenbuttel, and eagerly perused the adventures of the young Ascanius, a romantic history of the Chevalier Charles Edward's adventures in the year forty-five. I purchased this luckless hero's bust in plaster, which was at this time much sold in London. Indeed, so warm were the feelings of this young prince's partisans, that a wealthy squire in Staffordshire went so far as to clothe a fox in scarlet military coat, and hunt him with hounds clad in tartan.

I remembered what Anthony Grimshaw had told me of my father's sentiments on this subject, and was already at heart a staunch Jacobite. Nay, I think the frequent sight of those ghastly trophies on Temple Bar would in itself have been sufficient to inspire me with sedition. But in the character and fortunes of the Pretender there was an all-powerful magnet which drew to him the youth of the nation. What generous lad or sentimental woman would be faithful to an elderly German ruler while the brave young heart of an exiled prince was pining in obscurity, dependence, and banishment; and while the country from which he was excluded seemed to have gained so little by its ill-treatment of him ?

I had lived in London three months, and had eaten my Christmas dinner at a tavern in Fetter Lane. Once only had I heard from Lady Barbara, though I had written to her at the milliner's address several times. Her letter was long and kind. She gave much comfort and wise advice, but, alas ! little news of her whose name alone would to my eyes have shone upon the page as if written in starlight. Of my foster-father and his wife the charitable lady wrote with deep tenderness. Nothing had been heard of the poor runaway, and the hearts of father and mother were all but broken. Lady Barbara had been many times to see them. Sir Marcus and his family were to come to London in January, and then my dear benefactress said she would contrive to see me, though it must needs be by stealth.

From this letter I derived new comfort; to this promised meeting I looked forward with eager hope. Should I see *her* as well as Lady Barbara ? Alas! I knew that no good could come of any meeting between us two. But none the less eager was my longing—none the less sweet the dreams in which sleep restored my lost happiness, and I fancied that

Dora and I were seated side by side in the sunny window at Hauteville, with our books about us, as we had sat so often in the summer days that were gone.

It was while I was looking forward to the arrival of the family in St. James's Square, that a change took place in my mode of life, and the loneliness of my humble chambers was exchanged for company which I found sufficiently agreeable.

I had returned to my chambers late after treating myself to a sight of Shakspeare's *Romeo and Juliet*, which was then being played at the rival houses, at one Garrick and Miss Bellamy, at the other Barry and Mrs. Cibber, on which the wits declared that one saw at one house *Romeo and Juliet*, at the other *Juliet and Romeo*. Several distinguished members of Mr. Garrick's company had withdrawn themselves to Covent Garden, and there had been complaints made of him in a prologue, whereon Mrs. Clive replied sharply in an epilogue spoken by her at Drury Lane, and there was thus war between the patent theatres. It was to see Garrick that I had spent my shillings, and the delight afforded me by that great man's genius had amply repaid me for my extravagance.

It was black as Erebus on the staircase leading to my garret, but I was accustomed to the crazy old stair, and mounted quickly without tripping. But close by my own door I stumbled against some heavy body.

'Who is this?' I called out, surprised.

'A wretch who would be lying on a door-step in the open street if he were not sheltered here. You are new to London, Mr. Ainsleigh, and should have some spark of charity's divine warmth yet left in your heart. I crept here at dusk, thinking to find you at home, and have lain here in hiding ever since. Will you give me a supper and a night's shelter?'

'I would rather give you the money to pay for them,' I answered, 'since you and I are strangers.'

'That is your true London charity—alms given at arm's length,' replied the stranger with a sneer. 'I don't want your money, I want your friendship.'

I could see nothing of the man's face or figure in the darkness, but he spoke like a gentleman, or at least a man of some education.

'Come, Mr. Robert Ainsleigh,' he continued, 'you had best take me into your chambers, and strike a light. We shall understand one another better when we see each other's faces. I do not come to you as the first that offers, and a crown from you is not the same to me as another man's five shillings. For the last week I have been hanging about the Temple, where I was once a student-at-law, and have watched you come and go. I like your face. I feel an interest in you that I don't feel in other men, because you are beginning life pretty much as I began it, and with the same chances before you. You stand almost alone in the world, as I did, and you belong to a good old family, as I do.'

'How do you know all this?'

'From a clerk at Swinfen's, who remembers me when I was a gentleman. Come, Mr. Ainsleigh, you had better unlock your door and strike a light.'

I had no inclination whatever to admit this forward stranger into my rooms, but yielded weakly, because I knew not how to refuse. I opened my door, and the unknown followed close upon my heels, as if determined I should have no time to change my mind. When I had managed to light my solitary candle I turned and scrutinized this new acquaintance as closely as the feeble glimmer of the tallow-candle would allow me.

He was a man of from thirty to five-and-thirty years of age, with a face that had once been handsome, but which was prematurely worn by care or dissipation. He wore no wig, but his light-brown hair, plentiful at the back though his brow was bald, was tied with a greasy black ribbon. His clothes were of the shabbiest, but had once been fine. His eyes were gray, large, and penetrating; but I was at this time too bad a judge of countenance to perceive their sinister expression. As it was, however, his face did in nowise prepossess me, and when I too weakly yielded to him I was influenced by his conversation alone. He had groped for a chair while I lighted my candle, and sat by my cheerless hearth, shivering.

'Let me light your fire,' he cried, espying the fuel in a box by the rusty fender. 'I can make a fire as well as any Temple laundress, and cook a steak better than most of them.'

He suited the action to the word, and was on his knees piling up coals and firewood in the little grate before I could object.

'And now, Mr. Ainsleigh,' he said, flinging him-

M 2

self into a chair when the fire was lighted, 'let us talk reasonably. You are a solitary young man, just beginning the world, with fair prospects of success, and with, I have no doubt, a decent allowance from your aristocratic kinswoman.'

'What right have you to be so certain of my business?' I asked angrily.

'The right which knowledge of the world gives to every man who is not an arrant blockhead. I know you are living on money from your kinswoman by the left-hand——'

'Sir!'

'Pshaw! let us have no affectation of anger. What if I knew your father? I'll not say I did, but I know those who knew him. I know you are a dependent on the bounty of Lady Barbara Lestrange, and that you were turned out of doors by her husband.'

'Oblige me by carrying your knowledge elsewhere, sir. It is close upon midnight, and I do not care to be entertained with your version of my biography.'

'I want to show you that I am no flatterer, and that I can beg without licking the shoes of my patron. Come, Mr. Ainsleigh, you want a servant, and I want a master. Give me a closet to sleep in,

or let me lie on the mat at your door. You pay
your laundress something, and I will do her work
for nothing. I know more law than many a
prosperous counsellor, and can give you some help
in your studies if you will consent to take it from
such a vagabond as I. I can valet you, and cook
for you, run on your errands, and show you the
town, which I know by heart, and which is a pro-
founder science than you may fancy. I want a
shelter—and a friend.'

'Friendship is scarcely won by such means as
you employ.'

'Say, then, an acquaintance, a companion. Some
one fresh and young and true, with whom a battered
wretch may consort to the profit of his soul and
body. Mind you, Mr. Ainsleigh, I am a beggar to-
night, but not a beggar always. I suppose you have
heard of that notorious beast of burden, the bookseller's hack? That is my species. I have a prose
translation of Homer that I hope yet to turn into
cash, in a portmanteau in pawn at my last lodging.'

'From the Greek?'

'No; from Chapman. I know something of
Greek, too, but we bookmakers prefer adapting the
labours of a predecessor. I have also a history

of that strange extinct race the Amazons, which I think might tempt Mr. Cave, could I but approach him in a decent coat.'

It is needless to dwell longer on my conversation with this gentleman, whose persuasion ultimately prevailed with me. That he was a man of some education and had fallen from a better estate was very obvious; and this touched me, for I remembered that my father's condition must have much resembled that of this penniless stranger. And then common humanity pleaded for this unfortunate. Could I, who had been reared by charity, refuse a shelter and a crust to another? True, the man might be a rogue, but benevolence first feeds and clothes the reprobate, before it essays to reform him. Swayed by these considerations, I consented to share my lodgings with the stranger. I assisted him to make up a bed on the floor of my sitting-room, selected for him a few articles from my well-stocked wardrobe, and promised that, so long as he proved honest and I had money, he should not starve. And thus, on the very threshold of manhood, I suffered myself to be coaxed into an alliance with a vagabond, of whom I knew nothing save that he was impudent and persevering.

CHAPTER X.

WHEN I arose next morning, I found my breakfast comfortably prepared, the room swept and dusted, and the charwoman who had hitherto attended me dismissed, while my new acquaintance, dressed in the clothes I had given him, presented a decent, and even gentlemanlike appearance. He certainly had not exaggerated his handiness, for my room looked cleaner than ever it had done under the *régime* of my deaf laundress; and the steak which he had cooked for my breakfast might have gratified the senses of a Lucullus.

He would fain have breakfasted off the fragments of my own meal, but this I refused. If he was good enough to live with me, he was good enough to eat with me. I had a lurking consciousness that I had done a foolish thing, but felt that I could not amend my folly by a haughty treatment of my unknown companion. While we breakfasted, he gave me a brief sketch of his career and fortunes.

'My name is Philip Hay,' he began; 'and I am the son of a parson, a man of some learning, but a poor spirit, who spent his life in the seclusion of an agricultural district, neglected his flock while he read the classics, and brought up his family on the produce of his garden and pigstye. I can hardly remember wearing a shirt that was not ragged, or a coat and breeches that had not served my elder brother faithfully before they fell to my share. At our table butcher's meat was not the rule but the exception; and I am somewhat inclined to attribute my want of moral stamina to that deficiency of beef from which I suffered in my boyhood. Butcher's meat is the foundation of your true Englishman. I will not say that my father gave me a good education, for he suffered me to pick up the crumbs of his learning very much as the cocks and hens that stalked about our carpetless parlour at meal-times were accustomed to pick up the fragments of each repast. I may say without boastfulness, since my education has never been of the smallest use to me, that I had a natural aptitude for learning. Nothing in the way of scholarship came amiss to me. I knew my Greek alphabet before I was breeched, and read Erasmus in the original while other lads were blundering over their first declension. This early proficiency soon attracted the notice of neighbours, who, entirely unlearned themselves, were disposed to regard me as a juvenile prodigy; very much as they would have done had Nature gifted me with two heads, or enriched me with a superfluous arm. My reputation at twelve years old spread as far as the mansion of a wealthy nobleman, who sent for me one day when he had a house full of company, and bade me repeat an ode of Horace, and specimens of other classic poets, for the amusement of his guests. The result of this exhibition was an invitation to spend the holidays with my lord's son, an idle but by no means stupid young jackanapes, whom my learned example might possibly convert to industry. My father was but too glad to accept such an invitation; friends and neighbours declared that my fortune was made; my mother patched and turned the soundest of my old clothes, and my father pledged his credit to procure me the first suit of new ones I ever owned. I left home in high spirits, ingratiated myself at once with my patron's son, Viscount Escote, whom I was so fortunate, or so unfortunate, as to amuse, and whose friendship or fancy I was soon master of. With this young gentleman I spent the merriest, and indeed the happiest, period of my life, and the acqaintance thus begun was not destined to lapse. The boy had a warm heart, and I had perhaps reason to love him even better than I did.

'Lord Escote's tutor, a very grave and pompous gentleman, was at first inclined to object to his pupil's affection for my society, but as I speedily discovered this pedagogue's incompetency, and was able to pose him at any moment by a seemingly innocent inquiry about a crabbed line in Juvenal, or an obscure verb in Æschylus, he soon became more amiable, and permitted me to enjoy my share of those good things which he obtained by the exercise of grave humbug and sanctimonious imposture. When my lord went to the university, some four years after our first meeting, nothing would please him but I must go also; and his father, Lord Mallandaine, being by this time deceased, and he succeeded to the title, with no one but a foolish, indulgent mother to govern him, he of course had his way, and I enjoyed the education of a gentleman at my patron's charge.

'I could tell you rare stories of those wild days, Mr.

Ainsleigh, stories of exploits that redound rather to
my cleverness than to my patron's morality or my
own sense of honour. To sum up the whole, we
were both expelled the university under circumstances
of peculiar disgrace; and Lord Mallandaine, not
caring to face a doting mother, proposed a conti-
nental tour, with me for his companion. Together
we visited France, Italy, and the Low Countries,
intrigued with Venetian courtesans, and gamed with
Parisian dandies, got up cock-fights in the Colosseum
at Rome, and sparring-matches in a Florentine palace,
returned to England low in pocket and broken in
health, discontented with each other and disgusted
with the world. I happened fortunately to be master
of more than one important secret of my patron's, and
in consideration of this fact, rather than from any
remnant of his early friendship for me, my lord
presented me with a few hundreds, and bade me
make my fortune at the Bar, for which profession, he
was good enough to observe, my natural impudence
and capacity for lying eminently adapted me. I
thanked him in my politest manner, and cursing
him in spirit, wished him good-day. Since then
we have met rarely, and then only by accident,
and my chief consolation whilst going to the dogs

has been to know that he is treading the same road.'

'That is scarcely a Christian sentiment,' said I, 'since, by your own showing, Lord Mallandaine was kind to you.'

'Kind? yes! He kept me about him so long as I amused him, and kicked me off when he tired of me. You do not know—your simplicity cannot conceive—the things I have done for that man, the degradations to which I have submitted, the perils I have encountered. Believe me, Sganarelle's situation is no sinecure. And some day, in a brief fit of virtue, Don Juan turns away his faithful servant.'

'How came you to succeed so ill at the Bar?'

'You will understand that better ten years hence. I began steadily enough, and for the first two years ate my dinners and studied with a pleader; but the habit of dissipation was too strong upon me. I took to spending my night in gaming-houses, and even worse places of entertainment, brought discreditable company to my chambers, got into ill-repute with the Benchers, and it ended by my being kicked out of the Temple, as I had been kicked off by my patron, and as I had been expelled from my college. You perceive I have a genius for getting turned out of doors.'

'And since this time you have lived by literature?'

'I have lived by writing for the booksellers, if you call that literature: I don't. I have composed more biographies of lately defunct celebrities than I can count; have written a history of the Greek and Roman heroes, adapted for schools, and stolen from Plutarch; have composed metrical translations of such Latin poets as are least fit for publication; have invented a scandalous history of the Princess of Wales, whom I have no grounds for supposing anything but a very estimable matron; and have written pamphlets for and against every party. And now, sir, you know the worst of me. Upon my merits I have not presumed to touch; but even my enemies admit that I have an easy temper and a daring spirit, and that I can be a firm friend to the man who wins my regard. I have flung myself upon your charity, because I like your face; and it is for you to decide whether you will turn me out of doors, or allow me to remain as your faithful drudge and servitor until my luck turns, as it is sure to do in a week or two, when I will freely pay my share of our expenses, and continue truly grateful for your company.'

And now came my fatal moment of weakness. I was but just twenty, and easily won to pity the misfortunes of my fellow-men, however well-deserved might be their woes. The man's story was in every manner calculated to prejudice me against him; but I reflected that this very fact told in his favour, and was at least evidence of his candour, since it would have been easy for so clever a rascal to give a plausible account of himself. There seemed a reckless honesty about the fellow that fascinated me in spite of myself. How often had I felt the solitude of my chambers intolerable, and here was a learned and jovial companion eager to share them with me. True, that his character might be against him; but I had now begun the world, and must expect to encounter strange characters. And then, I doubt not that my vanity was tickled by his avowed fancy for me; and I suffered this adroit flattery to influence me in his favour. What chance has rustic youth against a citizen of the world such as this? The snare had been ingeniously prepared, and I walked blindfold into the meshes.

'I'll not turn you out of doors!' I cried heartily; 'and if you possess the learning for which you give yourself credit, I shall be very glad of your company.'

'Your hand on that,' said Philip Hay; 'and now that I am provided with a decent coat I'll go and look up Mr. Cave, and see if I can strike a bargain with him for my Amazons.'

On this he departed, and was no sooner gone than I began to ponder seriously whether this Mr. Hay would ever return, and if I had not been cheated out of a substantial suit of clothes by this eloquent adventurer. I had been warned against the tricks of the town, and this might be one of them. I laughed aloud as I thought how easily I had been cheated.

In this matter, however, I was agreeably disappointed. At five o'clock in the afternoon in comes my gentleman, with his hat cocked on one side, and his face triumphant.

'Look you there, Mr. Robert Ainsleigh!' he cried, flinging a purse of guineas on the table. 'Your clothes have brought me luck. Mr. Cave happened to be in rare good-humour to-day, and I have struck a very fair bargain for my history. There was a great hulking fellow, with a queer twitch of his face and limbs, hanging about the shop, who went near to spoil my market by the display of his learning. He cried out that the Amazons were fabulous

females, and that I could know as much of them as I
knew of Achilles—just what was told in Homer, and
fragmentary snatches of the Cyclic poets. But I
extinguished my twitching friend—who wore a coat
that was patched at the elbows and ragged at the
cuffs, showing at once premeditated poverty and
natural slovenliness—and talked Cave into an affection for my Amazons. Here are ten guineas earnest-
money, and by your leave, Mr. Ainsleigh, we'll
spend a pleasant evening. Shall it be at Marylebonne
Gardens or Don Saltero's, Ranelagh or Vauxhall?
Under which king, Bezonian?'

I would fain have avoided appearing in public with
my new acquaintance, of whom I knew nothing that
was not to his discredit; but his good-humour and
joviality soon vanquished my scruples. I had a
natural curiosity about the pleasures of the town,
those dazzling scenes of riot and delight which I had
heard so praised by my fellow-students in the
dining-hall—the places not to know which was
to be in some manner behind the age. In a
word, I suffered Mr. Philip Hay to lead me
where he pleased; and those evenings which had
hitherto been spent in the studious quiet of my
chamber, or the grave gossip of an obscure coffee-

house, were now given entirely to the pleasures of the town.

I might perhaps have continued to regard Philip Hay's assumed affection for myself with doubt and suspicion if that reprobate individual had required anything from me. But his fortunes revived from the first day of our acquaintance, and he was more extravagant in his expenditure than myself, notwithstanding that my purse had been replenished by a bank-note enclosed in Lady Barbara's last letter. He reproached me loudly for my parsimony when I refused to drink or game in the vivacious company to which he introduced me at Vauxhall and other public places; and on more than one occasion, by his somewhat scornful offers to pay my score, drew me into an outlay which I afterwards regretted; for I never forgot that I owed all to my benefactress, and the natural pride of manhood was only sustained by the hope that I should one day be able to repay all.

Nor were my nights spent in noisy pleasure at Don Saltero's, or wasted in the Ranelagh Rotundo, unattended by the after-bitterness of remorse. From scenes so frivolous, from company so loose and unprincipled, my thoughts went back to Hauteville,

the calm days and happy evenings, the pleasant con-
versations over my lady's tea-board, the summer
sunsets Dorothea Hemsley and I had watched from
the Italian garden, when the night-dews hung heavy
on the roses, and the last of midsummer's nightingales
sang loud in the dusky distance of the wood. But,
in spite of these better thoughts, the pleasures into
which my companion plunged me were not without
their charm. The restraint in which my boyhood
had been spent especially fitted me to be the fool of
such frivolous temptations: and my Mephistopheles
contrived his snares with a rare genius. Seldom did
he suffer weariness to mar my amusement. A skilful
courtier, set on by wily ministers to lure a crown-prince
from thoughts of statecraft into the vile slough of
dissipation, could not have acted his part with greater
care or wisdom. In a word, my tempter played upon
me as Prince Hamlet bade the courtiers play upon
'this pipe;' and it was only afterwards, when I
saw the other side of his cards, that I knew the
subtlety of his game, and how utterly helpless I had
been in his hands.

I had enjoyed the privilege of Mr. Hay's society
for six weeks before Sir Marcus Lestrange and his
family came to London. I had ventured to call

more than once in St. James's Square, where the
house-porter informed me that his master was suffering from an attack of gout, which detained him at
Hauteville, and that Mr. Lestrange was in Paris. I
was relieved to hear of Everard's absence, and to
know that Dora was for the present free from the
attention, or persecution, of her enforced suitor.

We came through St. James's Square one night,
after an evening spent at Vauxhall, whence it had
pleased us to return on foot. I have since had
reason to believe that Mr. Hay had his own special
purpose in bringing me this way on this particular
night. We had supped with some of his rackety
acquaintance at the gardens, and he had induced
me to drink a little more than usual. The punch,
the company, and the long walk in the night-air
had combined to excite my brain, and for the first
time during our acquaintance I had spoken freely
of my friends at Hauteville; nor did I perceive
until afterwards, when considering my night's folly
in the sober reflections of the next morning, how
artfully my companion led me on to the revelation
of my most secret thoughts.

The windows of Sir Marcus's house were blazing
with the light of numberless candles as we came

into the square. The family had arrived, and Lady
Barbara was holding a reception. The great hall-
door was open, and we saw the splendour within,
with guests ascending and descending, and footmen
bawling in the hall and on the staircase. Without
there was a crowd of chair-men, footmen with flaring
torches, link-boys, and lantern-bearers, though it
was a fine spring night, and the stars shining high
up in the clear cold gray. We stood to watch the
company passing in and out, powder and diamonds,
rustling trains of gorgeous hues, and gold and
silver brocade, that flashed in the glare of the
torches. The crowd proclaimed the names of
beaux and belles, soldiers and statesmen. Now
there was a hush and murmur in the crowd as Mr.
Pelham descended from his chariot, with ribbon
and star upon his breast, and a smile upon his
florid countenance. How soon was that respected
head to be laid low! And here, close behind him,
came the Duke of Newcastle, looking right and left,
with his glass held affectedly to his eye, challenging
the plaudits of the crowd.

'What a grinning baboon goes yonder!' cried my
companion, who knew every one; 'it is a monkey that
clambers into power on the shoulders of better men.'

A thick-set, clumsy-looking man, with a dark scowling face, came presently through the crowd.

'Yonder goes the Secretary of War, Henry Fox,' said Mr. Hay; 'one of the greatest statesmen we have, but not eloquent as a speaker. Did you ever see such a hang-dog countenance? One would say 'twas a fellow that had just committed a murder and hid the body in a ditch. But the man is a genius! If he and Pitt could but combine their forces, the brotherhood of Pelham must bow their diminished heads. Sir Marcus is well in with the Ministry, you see, and I doubt not will get some new berth abroad or at home. Why, with such interest, you ought to be in the House of Commons, instead of slaving for the reward of a shabby stuff gown, and the right to cross-examine the witnesses for the crown against a sheepstealer! But come away; it is sorry pleasure hanging about the door when we feel ourselves good enough for the best company in the drawing-room.'

'I am not so sure of my own merits as you are of yours, Philip,' I answered, laughing; 'but there is one in that house I would give a great deal to see.'

'And that one is Miss Dorothea Hemsley, a

young lady with fifty thousand pounds for her fortune, who is engaged to her cousin Everard Lestrange, and who would marry you to-morrow if you had the courage of a mouse!' said my companion.

We had now drawn a little aloof from the crowd; Philip Hay had thrust his arm through mine, and was leading me homewards.

'What do you mean?' I cried, aghast at such sacrilege as this light mention of a name that was, and has ever been, sacred to my ears.

'I mean that I am a man of the world, and know what stuff women are made of. You tell me that Miss Hemsley is plighted, or all but plighted, to young Lestrange, as hardened a sinner as my late patron Mallandaine, from whom I have heard his character. And you have watched her, and seen her unhappy; and you surprised her once in tears; and she owned that the burden of her sorrow was hard to bear. Yet with all her sorrow she found time and patience to teach you Spanish, and was pleased you should polish her Italian; and sang with you, and walked with you, and watched with a face white as a corpse while Sir Marcus reviled and banished you, and sent you a little pious monkish book for your comfort. Why, man alive, the woman loves you—'tis plain as the nose on your face—and would marry you out of hand if you had the spirit to ask her.'

'That is impossible—even if I could do such an act of dishonour against Lady Barbara, which I could not. Those who have authority over her would take care to prevent such a marriage.'

'Yes, if you were so dull a blockhead as to ask their permission. But I don't suppose even your rustic simplicity is simple enough for that. There are parsons by the score in May Fair and the Fleet who will marry you without leave or license from parents and guardians; and you will surely not let the young lady be sacrificed to a man she hates for lack of a little courage on your part.'

'If daring of mine could secure her happiness, there are few perils I would not dare,' I answered boldly.

'Pshaw! thou art a creature of ifs and buts. Had I such good fortune as to win the heart of an orphan heiress, I would not stand shivering on the door-step while my lady-love was pining for me within.'

The cold night and the walk had sobered me by

this time, and the man's tone offended me. I begged him to trouble himself no more about my business, which I assured him I could conduct without his advice. He received my rebuff with his usual good-humour, and for some time forbore to offend by any mention of Dora's name.

CHAPTER XI.

WE PLIGHT OUR TROTH.

On the following day I received a note from Lady Barbara. It had been written before the assembly of the previous night, and it informed me that the writer would walk in the Mall in St. James's Park at three o'clock the next afternoon, attended only by a footman, and would be pleased if I could join her there, as if by accident.

Philip Hay was present when I received this letter, and soon after proposed an expedition that would occupy the afternoon and evening. When I declined this he questioned me so closely that I confessed I was going to meet my patroness. He congratulated me on being so high in her favour, and went out upon his own business.

My heart beat high as I entered the Mall. If Dora should be with Lady Barbara!—if!—but I knew this could not be. My lady herself had been anxious to banish me from that sweet society, and would she again expose me to the danger which had already well-nigh wrecked my peace? No; I felt sure my benefactress would be alone; and yet it was with a pang of disappointment I saw her solitary figure approach me.

It was not the fashionable hour for promenaders, and except for an occasional passer, or a strolling nurse-girl with her brood of children, we had the walk well-nigh to ourselves.

Lady Barbara dismissed her footman, bidding him return for her in half an hour. She led the way to a retired seat under one of the newly budding elms, and here we sat side by side, my lady for a few moments silent with emotion, and I no less deeply moved.

Presently she took my hand and kissed it.

'Dear Robert! dear adopted son!' she murmured gently, 'it is hard to meet you thus by stealth.'

'Nothing is hard to me, dear madam, except the loss of your affection.'

'And that loss can never happen to you. I have only to look in your face, and the past comes back to me, and I fancy you are your father, and I am young, and jealous, and wicked, and miserable once more.

No justice that I can do to you will atone for that old wrong to him. Oh, if it could! But that is a vain wish; a wrong done to the dead is done for ever. How well you look! how manly you have grown! You had never much of the rustic air, but even that you had is gone, and you are a courtier, a man of the world. In what school have you been graduating?'

I blushed as I bethought myself that it was in those notorious seminaries of Ranelagh and Vauxhall I had acquired the manly air on which my dear lady was pleased to congratulate me.

'Speak to me of yourself, dear madam,' I said, 'and of——'

'And of Dora!' said Lady Barbara, as I paused confused. 'Ah, Robert, that is a business which sorely troubles me.'

'What business, madam?'

'Dora's marriage with Everard. As the time draws near I begin to doubt the wisdom of my husband's conduct in this matter.'

'As the time draws near!' I cried, my heart beating painfully. 'What do you mean by those words, madam?'

'Ah, I forgot! You know nothing of what has happened since you left Hauteville. Sir Marcus has hurried on this marriage between his niece and his son. I fear he has pressed his suit somewhat too persistently. The dear child yields, but I am sure she is unhappy; and oh! Robert, I sorely fear it is for her fortune Everard is so eager.'

'I know as much, Lady Barbara,' replied I, and proceeded to repeat the remarks on this subject with which Mr. Everard had favoured me. 'No man who loved a woman would speak of her thus,' I said in conclusion.

On this my lady became very thoughtful.

'Oh, Robert, would to Heaven I knew what is best to be done!' she cried after a pause.

'Anything is better than that Miss Hemsley should be unhappy,' said I; 'and I do not believe *that* marriage can result in her happiness. Oh, madam, believe me, this is no selfish argument! It is not because I love her that I say this. Alas! what hope have I? Sever her from Everard Lestrange to-morrow, and she is no nearer me. But why should her peace be sacrificed to any ambitious design of her guardian's?'

'It was her father's wish also, Robert. Mr. Hemsley was a rich city merchant, who owed his position in society to his alliance with the Lestranges. He had a great friendship for my husband, and it

WE PLIGHT OUR TROTH.

was he who first mooted the idea of Dorothea's union with her cousin. His will was made with a view to this; and if Dora marries without her guardian's consent, she forfeits half of her fifty thousand pounds, which sum goes to Sir Marcus.'

I was inexpressibly glad to hear this; it seemed to lessen by one-half the distance between the heiress and me.

'Ah, madam, how happy the lover who should win her against her uncle's will!' cried I.

'Even then she would have no despicable fortune. The stringent terms of Mr. Hemsley's will are by no means singular in days when clandestine marriages are so common, and an heiress the mark for every adventurer. There is some talk of a bill to stop Fleet marriages; but they say Henry Fox will oppose it with all his might, since he owes his happiness to a stolen match.'

'You spoke of Miss Hemsley's marriage as near at hand, madam. When is it to be?'

I faltered, and found myself cowering like one who awaits his death-blow.

'Alas! Robert, very soon; in a few weeks.'

'That is indeed soon. But surely, madam, if this young lady does not love her cousin you will interfere to prevent her misery ? If Sir Marcus be the guardian of her fortune, you are as surely the proper guardian of her peace ; you cannot consent to see her sacrificed.'

'I know not what I ought to do, Robert,' replied my lady, helplessly ; 'I wish I better knew the dear girl's heart ; and yet I dare not question her. I have tried my uttermost to dissuade Sir Marcus from this hasty marriage ; but he is inflexible. And Dora is *his* niece and ward, not mine. Everard is in Paris, where he is appointed Secretary of Legation ; but he comes back to-morrow night. He is on the road at this moment, and the preparations for the wedding are already begun. The milliners are busy with the bride's finery ; but the poor child takes no pleasure in laces and brocades. I remember the fuss about my own wedding-clothes, and what weary work it all seemed to me. Ah, Robert, these loveless, joyless marriages must surely be displeasing to Heaven. But I see my servant coming back to us. You must go, dear ; I shall write to you soon. Good-bye, and God bless you ! '

So we parted ; I to return to the Temple, sorely depressed in spirits. Nor were Mr. Hay's persuasions of any avail with me for some time after this.

The very thought of crowded public gardens filled me with aversion; I sickened at my comrade's boisterous jokes; I buried myself in my books, and would have given much to be rid of this old man of the mountain, who had contrived to fasten himself upon my shoulders. I think Mr. Hay's tact enabled him to perceive this; for he left me to myself for upwards of a week soon afterwards, absenting himself upon his own business, as he said.

Days and weeks passed, and brought me no letter from Lady Barbara. I suffered tortures of anxiety, and every evening after dark stole away from my books and walked to St. James's Square, where, under cover of the friendly night, I reconnoitred the mansion that sheltered Dorothea Hemsley. The lighted windows, more or less brilliantly illuminated, told me nothing of her who was perhaps sad and sorrowful within. Sometimes the thought that she was being forced into a hateful marriage went nigh to drive me to desperation. I remembered what Philip Hay—that soldier of fortune and citizen of the world—had said to me. The great doors of the diplomatist's house stood open before me. Why should I not rush in and rescue my darling from her oppressors by force of arms—my own strong arms, which should be able to shield and save her from all

the world? Why should I not do this? Why,
indeed, except that I had no right to suppose such
a proceeding would be agreeable to Miss Hemsley.
Could I have been assured of her love, there would
have been little need of hesitation. But how was I,
the least learned of students in the science of
woman's heart, to interpret, with any certainty,
tender looks, and gentle blushes, and downcast eyelids, and faint fluttering hand, and low tremulous
voice? Those sweet signs of maiden bashfulness
might mean so little—or so much.

One night that I found the house in St. James's
Square dimly lighted, and the porter standing at the
open door tasting the evening air, I made so bold as
to ask that functionary whether there was not soon
to be a marriage in the family he served. The man
had not been at Hauteville, being no doubt too burly
and ponderous a person for removal from his leather-
hooded chair in London, and I therefore ran no
hazard of recognition.

Yes; he informed me that on Thursday fortnight
the young lady of the house was to be married.
The blow struck hard. Thursday fortnight! It
was now Tuesday; in sixteen days Dora would be
gone from me for ever.

I returned to my chambers with a distracted

mind, but happily found a brief note from Lady Barbara awaiting me.

'We shall be at Vauxhall to-morrow evening,' she wrote; 'be sure to be at ten o'clock in the dark walk to the right of the statue of Neptune,—and be cautious. We shall not be alone.'

'We.' Did 'we' mean my Lady and Miss Hemsley? I thought as much; and I know not how I lived till the next night. Philip Hay's presence and lively interest in my welfare seemed at this time particularly obtrusive. He questioned me closely as to where I was going to spend my evening, and said he had made a special appointment for me with some friends of his own at Vauxhall.

I doubt not that some movement of vexation at this intelligence betrayed where I was going, if he had not the knowledge already from another source.

Evening came, and I found myself for the first time alone in the gardens, fluttered with unspeakable hopes, and very anxious to avoid any encounter with Mr. Philip Hay. Though I had meant to arrive only a few minutes before the hour named by Lady Barbara, it was but nine o'clock when I entered the gates, so swiftly did my desires outrun time. I kept entirely to the dark walks, and looked at my watch every time I came to a solitary lamp. Every footstep fluttered me, every rustle of brocade set my heart beating with a sudden tumult. I thought the gardens could never have been so full of fops and belles, the dark alleys never so affected by the company.

At last the clock struck ten; the distant music grew confused in my ears; placid stars above and lamps below swam before my eyes. Two ladies in hoods and masks approached, and in another moment Dora was at my side.

'Dora—Miss Hemsley!' I faltered; and then I know not what impulse possessed me, but, forgetful of all except the delight of this meeting, I clasped the dear girl in my arms. 'My love, my darling!' I cried, 'this hateful marriage must not be.'

'No, Robert,' she murmured, gently withdrawing herself from my embrace, 'it shall not be. I have been very weak and cowardly; but when the time drew near, despair made me bold, and I cast myself upon Lady Barbara's mercy. Dearest aunt! she is all goodness, and she will not suffer me to be wretched for life, as I should be if I married one I cannot love, whom I cannot even respect.'

'Yes, Robert,' said my lady, 'we must save this dear girl. I knew not her heart till the night before last, when some tearful words she let fall tempted me to question her. We must save her—but how? I cannot openly oppose the will of her guardian, my husband; and I *know* nothing against my stepson. It is a faithful lover must save her, Robert.'

My lady and Dora had both removed their masks. The sweet girl stood before me, one moment pale as a lily, and in the next blushing crimson.

' There is one, madam, who would shrink from no dangerous service if he might be permitted to save her, and who would take her for his wife penniless more proudly than as heiress to a great fortune. But he is obscure, dependent, almost nameless.— Would you not despise such an one, Dora? '

'Despise you!' faltered my angel tenderly; and she gave me a divine look from her blue eyes.

'I begin to think I am not wanted here,' cried my lady, laughing; ' I will go and pay my respects to Neptune.—Ah, Dora, will you hang your pearl necklace on the sea-god's trident if you escape shipwreck on life's troubled ocean? '

She was gone. I led my darling to a bench, and we sat down side by side. She put on her mask again; was it to hide those maiden blushes? And then, emboldened by sudden joy, I spoke to her of my love, and implored her to consent to a speedy clandestine marriage.

'I would not offer you a name so obscure, Dora,' said I, when I had pleaded in swift passionate words that came from the very depth of my heart; 'I would rather wait and work patiently till I was worthier so dear a partner. But by this way only, or by a resolute refusal on your part, which would expose you to all the tortures of domestic persecution, can your union with Everard Lestrange be avoided; and oh, my darling, I think I would sooner see you dead than united to that man, for I know he is a villain. Who else should have forged the vile letter that banished and disgraced me? Who else should be privy to poor Margery's flight? Ah, Dora, *you* know how little of my time was spent at the warrener's lodge after one dear person came to Hauteville. I was but too forgetful of my old humble friends. No, darling, you must not marry Everard Lestrange. But can you consent to share a lot so lowly as mine?'

'Yes, Robert,' she whispered; and for a few blessed moments we sat silent, with clasped hands. This was our betrothal.

A faint rustling of the bushes behind startled us. I sprang to my feet.

'Who is there?' I cried, with my hand on my sword-hilt, for I was inclined to suspect an eavesdropper.

Again I heard a stealthy rustling, and swift footsteps in the next walk. I examined the hedge, which grew thick and high; but the listener, if there had been one, was gone. Those rapid retreating footsteps were his, no doubt.

Lady Barbara came hurrying towards us.

'Come, children,' she cried, 'is all settled?'

'There is nothing settled, dear madam, except that Miss Hemsley has blessed a most unworthy creature with her love.'

'Oh, Robert, if I can read you aright, she will have no cause to repent her confidence. Dear children! But there is not time for another word. We are here with a party, you know, Robert, and have stolen away from them. Our friends will be looking for us. Am I to arrange everything? Yes, I suppose mine is the only cool head among us. I will write to you, Robert.'

'Lady Barbara!' called a gentleman, running towards us.

'See, here comes Mr. Dolford, one of our beaux! Away with you, cousin, away!'

I pressed Dora's hand, murmured a blessing upon my cousin and my love, and vanished as my lady's cavalier approached her, complaining bitterly of her absence.

'We have all been hunting you, ladies. Delavanti, the conjuror, is just beginning his wonderful performance. It is the best thing to be seen this year, and I would not have you miss it.—Lestrange has been positively distracted, I protest, Miss Hemsley.'

I felt like a creature in a dream after leaving Dora. My head swam with the sweet intoxication of so much happiness. I could not tear myself from the garden, but hung about the darker walks in the faint hope of seeing her again. It was not till after midnight that I left the pleasure-haunt and walked eastwards under the pale April stars.

CHAPTER XII.

I AM TRAPPED BY A TRAITOR.

AFTER that too happy meeting at Vauxhall my spirits were too much distracted for the common business of life, and I found the society of Mr. Hay far from agreeable. I longed to be alone with my hopes and anxieties, but knew not how to get rid of a companion who cost me nothing, and took pains to make himself useful and necessary to me. In telling him what I had told him of my secrets, I had given him some right to be interested in my affairs, and this privilege he used with much freedom, and to my extreme annoyance, until I lost my temper one day, and informed him that I preferred to manage my own business without his advice or interference.

If I had hoped to rid myself of him by this means I was doomed to disappointment. Mr. Hay was blessed with an imperturbable temper, and an easy impudence not to be disconcerted by any rebuff.

'That's wrong, Bob,' he replied; 'the advice of a man of the world is always worth having; and I'll wager I could help you to a wife and a fortune if you'd let me.'

'I have no doubt of your genius for intrigue,' I answered coldly; 'but how is it you have not found those blessings for yourself?'

'How do you know that I have not had and lost them? A man of my stamp runs through a fortune, and quarrels and parts company from a wife, while a fellow of your icy nature is deliberating a love-letter.'

During this period of anxious expectation I found it impossible to rid myself of my companion's observation. If I went out after dark to watch the house that held my treasure, as I did every evening, he guessed my errand, and upbraided me for my pusillanimity. I tried to quarrel with him; but, as it did not suit the gentleman's purpose that we should part, I found this impossible.

It was a week after my meeting with Dora, and it seemed an age, when a visitor came to my chambers, and the door being opened by Mr. Hay, that person

appeared before me in high spirits, to announce
that a young woman wanted to speak to me.

'She is dressed like a milliner's girl or a lady's-
maid,' he said; 'but I'll wager it is thy inamorata
in disguise.'

I flew to the door, and found Miss Hemsley's
maid, a young Frenchwoman, whom I had seen
often at Hauteville, and who was no especial favourite of mine. She had a pinched, sallow countenance, with small piercing black eyes. She spoke
English very tolerably, but with an unpleasant nasal
twang, and I had heard Lady Barbara extol her as a
model of industry and fidelity. I felt, therefore,
that my own dislike of the girl was an unworthy
prejudice of the masculine mind, which is ever apt
to associate an unpleasing face with an inferior
nature. To-day I could have hugged Ma'amselle
Adolphine, so delighted was I to welcome any one
who brought me tidings of Dora. I led her into
my sitting-room, where Mr. Hay was lounging over
a newspaper.

'As this young woman has come to speak of
private business, I should be very glad to have
the room to ourselves for half an hour, Hay,'
said I.

'With all my heart, Bob; I can read the news at a coffee-house as well as here.—Your servant, madam.'

Mr. Hay saluted my visitor with a profound bow, and favoured her with a significant glance which I at the moment took for a simple fashionable leer, much affected at a time when your spurious fine gentleman's language to women was always spiced with double meaning, and his every look a declaration. I saw Mr. Hay safe outside my door, and then turned eagerly to the Frenchwoman.

'Now, Adolphine, what news from your mistress?' I cried. 'Have you brought me a letter?'

'Ah, mais, but no, monsieur!' shrieked the girl; 'mademoiselle is too well watch for that. She cannot run the hazard of to write. It is nothing but drums, and dinners, and masquerades, and picture-sales, and parties to Ranelagh all the day and all the night, and he, Monsieur Everard, is alway there—alway upon her steps. Mais, but it is my Lady Barbara who send me to-day. The marriage that you know of is to take place at once, at the Fleet, at May Fair, anywhere that they will ask no question. And if you have a friend who can help you to arrange the things, my Lady Barbara says—ah, let me not forget what it is she has said—since you know not the town, you are to confide in your friend, *pourvu* that you can trust yourself to him."

A friend ? What friend had I ? There was my companion, Mr. Philip Hay, clever, unscrupulous, practised in intrigue, and only too eager to be useful. But could I venture to confide my happiness to him ?

'What next, Adolphine ?' I cried.

'The marriages must be immediatement, see you, Monsieur Robert. This day week is fix for the wedding wid Monsieur Everard. To-night there is masquerade at Ranelagh. Mademoiselle will be there, with my Lady Barbara and Monsieur Eve-rard. At half-past twelve o'clock, when the rooms are most crowd, she will complain of the heat, and will retire to the cloak-room wid her aunt, where she will slip a black silk domino over her dress and will come out to the portico, alway wid her aunt. You must be upon the spot wid a hackney-coach ready to carry her away. It must all be done quick like the lightning, for Monsieur Everard will not be slow to take alarm ; and then you will drive at once to your parson, and he will marry you *sur-le-champ*. And after, you had best to leave the country with your bride, says my Lady Barbara, if you would not have the blood to be shed between you and Monsieur Everard.'

' I can protect my wife and my honour in England or elsewhere,' I answered proudly; and then with a throbbing heart I sat down to write to my dear girl, assuring her of my gratitude and love, and thanking her a thousand times for her confidence; a long, wild, rambling epistle I doubt not. I had not time to read it over, for the French-woman was in haste to be gone, so I crammed the letter and a couple of guineas into her hand and dismissed her.

When she was gone I paced my chamber thoughtfully for some time, debating the prudence of confiding in Philip Hay. After serious reflection I decided in his favour. True that I knew him to be a rascal, yet if well paid for his fidelity he would surely be faithful. And what interest could he have in betraying me? Some help in this matter I must assuredly have. I knew nothing of Fleet marriages or the law relating to them; and there was no time for me to obtain such knowledge from

strangers. I had often enough been hustled in Hol-
born and on Ludgate Hill by low wretches touting for
those reprobate parsons who made a living by such
clandestine unions ; but I could at least trust Philip
Hay rather than one of these vulgar adventurers. To
arrange a marriage between midnight and sunrise,
might be, nay, no doubt would be, a matter of some
difficulty ; and for this I needed just such help as my
companion could give me ; while, in the event of any
pursuit on the part of Everard Lestrange, the assistance of such a sturdy henchman would be of no small
service. It was already late in the afternoon, and
there was little time for indecision ; so I determined
on trusting Mr. Hay with this precious secret, and
on his return hastened to make him my confidant.

' It is just such an adventure as I love !' he cried
gaily. ' Leave all to me, and I will engage that the
soberest parson in the purlieus of the Fleet prison
shall be in waiting with book and gown to unite
you to your heiress at the unearthly hour of one to-
morrow morning. He will ask an extra fee for the un-
usual hour, though it is scarcely so uncommon as you
may think ; but of course you'll not object to that.'

' And will such a marriage be strictly legal ?' I
asked.

'Faith yes, Bob; the Gordian knot shall be as tight as if an archbishop had the tying of it—unless, indeed, you give special notice to the parson before-hand, when these ecclesiastics have a way of forget-ting to read some essential bit of the service, which omission enables Signor Sposo to bid Signora Sposa good-morning some fine day when she grows trouble-some.   Oh, they are rare obliging fellows, I assure you, these parsons ; but though these marriages are legal enough, it is a felony on their part to perform them, for which they are liable to prosecution.   But they snap their fingers at Mr. Justice, and contrive to live a jolly life.   There was Dr. Gainham, for instance, playfully entitled Bishop of Hell, a rare impudent dog ; and the famous Keith, who made a handsome fortune by his chapel in Mayfair ; and when there was some talk of his brother ecclesiastics putting down his traffic, vowed if they did he would buy a piece of ground and outbury them.'

While my companion rattled on thus, I was medi-tating my plans for the night.   Yes, Lady Barbara was right.   It would be best to carry my bride from England, and place her where she would be safe from Everard Lestrange's persecution.   I could come back to my native shores to fight him, if my

honour should demand such an act; but my first
thought must be of Dora.

I had luckily upwards of a hundred pounds in
hand; and this, after feeing Mr. Hay with a twenty-
pound note, would leave me plenty for a journey to
France, and a month or two's living in some pleasant rustic retreat, which Dora, who knew the
Continent, should choose. 'And I will be her
slave, and lie at her feet, during the brief happy
holiday of our honeymoon,' I thought; 'and then I
will come back to London and work for a position at
the Bar, and redeem my name from the stigma of
the fortune-hunter, and every penny of the income
from her five-and-twenty thousand pounds shall be
spent on herself, so that she may forget she is married to a poor man.'

My fancy flew to a pretty rural cottage I had seen
to let in one of the lanes beyond Kensington, during
a recent ramble in that quarter, and which I imagined
just such a simple paradise as my love would like.

'I will send Hay to secure it to-morrow,' I said to
myself, 'while Dora and I are posting towards Dover,
and I will ask Lady Barbara to furnish it for us.

Mr. Hay departed in search of a sober parson, and
to order the post-horses and chariot to convey us to

Dover; while I busied myself with the packing of a trunk to take with me on my journey. Never had I been so particular about my toilette. I deliberated solemnly between a blue suit and a chocolate one, and no elegant trifler of Pall Mall could have been more particular than I in my selection of cravat and ruffles.

By the time I had made my arrangements and counted my money, Mr. Hay returned. He had settled everything most pleasantly—found an exemplary parson, a real Oxford man, without a fault except a capacity for losing money at faro, at the tavern of the ' Two Sawyers,' Fleet Lane. The chaise and horses were ordered, and would be in waiting close to this place of entertainment.

' And by to-morrow noon you will be in Dover,' said my coadjutor, ' in time for the packet that sails at four in the afternoon, wind and weather permitting. And now let us go and dine together. What, man alive!' he cried, in answer to a dissentient look of mine, ' will you refuse to crack a bottle with a faithful friend at parting? By ——, Mr. Bob, unless I am used as a friend I will have no hand in this business. I am no dirty tool, too base to touch, but not too vile to use!'

'It was no want of friendship that made me hesitate, Phil,' I replied; 'but I am in too anxious a mood for pleasure, and shall be poor company. We'll have a bottle together, notwithstanding.'

I looked at my watch, a bulky Tompion with a clumsy outer case of leather, that had belonged to my grandfather the colonel, and had been flung aside as old-fashioned by my father when he went to Cambridge, and left in a drawer at Hauteville, where Lady Barbara found it, and gave it to me. It was early yet, and indeed, but for Mr. Hay's invitation to dine, I know not how I should have got rid of the hours that must pass before my appointment at Ranelagh.

My officious friend took me to a tavern that was strange to me, a house in Chelsea, where he ordered an excellent dinner, and so much wine that I remonstrated with him for his folly. But he informed me that we were not going to dine alone, and presently arrived a person of military aspect, in a uniform which I had never seen before, whom Mr. Hay introduced as Serjeant O'Blagg of the East India Company's service, a gentleman who thought no more of storming a Mahratta fortress than of cracking a bottle of burgundy, and who stood high in the estimation of Major Lawrence.

This brave warrior, whose Hibernian accent was in nowise modified by long service in the East, favoured us during dinner with many wonderful stories of his adventures in those distant lands, and dilated with a somewhat florid eloquence upon the wealth and glory to be won there.

'You gentlemen who know no more of war than those petty European skirmishes about which you kick up such a row, with firing of big guns and ringing of big bells, bedad, for a victory that you're neither better nor worse for, except in the matter of a new tax on our boots, or your wig, or your tay, ye've no notion of our conquests out yonder, where, at the sack of a town, there's diamonds as big as beans to be picked up in the streets, and the pearls fly as thick as hailstones about our soldiers' heads; and there's big brazen idols in the temples with their stomachs full of rubies and emeralds and such like, just as you stuff a Michaelmas goose, sir, and him as splits the haythen image asunder with the butt-end of his gun gets the stuffing for his pains. Why, the Great Mogul has seven golden thrones—or maybe some of 'em's silver—covered with jewels '—the ser-

geant called them 'jools'—'every one of 'em handsomer than t'other, except the one that's called the
paycock throne, and that whops the lot, and is valued
at forty millions of rupays.'

So he ran on, to the apparent delight of my companion, but to my own unutterable weariness. What
were the jewelled thrones of the Great Mogul to me,
who knew but one treasure, and sighed but for ono
dear prize? The sergeant's company vexed me; but
Philip Hay explained to me in an undertone that he
had met this old friend by accident in the street, and
could not well avoid asking him to join us at dinner.
I observed that the soldier drank ferociously, and
both he and Hay pressed the wine on me; but this
kindness I for some time resolutely declined. I
would have given much to have been away from these
boisterous boon-companions, and heartily repented
my confidence in Mr. Hay, which had placed me in
such an unwelcome position.

I gave but little attention to the sergeant's stories,
which he told in a noisy, uproarious manner peculiar
to the lower orders of his countrymen, and garnished
with military oaths. My thoughts were far away
from that boisterous table. When the bottle was
pushed towards me, with clamorous protestations

against my abstinence, I filled my glass mechanically, and in this manner when the night grew late I had drunk some three or four glasses of a claret which seemed to me a thin poor wine, ill-adapted to steal a man's brains. Yet by ten o'clock I felt a kind of stupor creeping over me—a confusion of the brain, in which the strident voice of the Irish soldier roaring his braggart stories of Indian conquest and loot, of Dupleix and the Great Mogul, peacock thrones, and royal elephants in jewelled harness, seemed strange and distant to my ears.

In this condition of my mind I was perpetually troubled by the idea that I had no right to be here. It was in vain that I looked at my watch, which showed me that I had nearly three hours to wait before my presence would be required at the gates of Ranelagh. At last I started up from the table in haste, telling Philip Hay that I could stay no longer, and if he was not ready to accompany me, would go alone.

He pointed to an eight-day clock in a corner of the room.

'Art thou mad, Bob?' he cried; 'it has not yet gone the half-hour after ten. Drink a glass of this rare old Hollands, and take things easy.'

He forced a glass of spirit upon me, which I drank
unwillingly enough.   It had a strange burning taste,
and I had reason afterwards to know that it was no
such simple liquor as Hollands I was thus made to
drink, but a dram doctored with an Indian spirit that
maddens the brain.

'We can get rid of the sergeant in half an hour,
and then go out and get our hackney-coach,' whispered Hay close in my ear.   'There is no need for
him to know our business.'

I acknowledged the wisdom of this, and tried to
listen with some degree of patience to the soldier's
long-winded stories, and my friend's comments upon
them ; but before I had listened long, the voices of
the two mingled confusedly, then grew to a buzzing
sound, and at last died away into a low murmur,
like the pleasant rustling of trees on a summer afternoon, as my head sank forward on the table, and I
slept.

I was awakened suddenly by a violent slap on the
shoulder, and a loud voice crying,—

'Twelve o'clock, Bob ; the landlord is shutting his
doors, and 'tis time we went in search of our coach.
Why, what a dull companion thou hast been !'

I staggered to my feet.   My eyeballs burnt, and

my head ached to splitting; for a moment I scarce remembered where I was, or the events of the day.

'Heavens, I have slept!' I exclaimed at last; 'and Dora waiting for me, perhaps. Why, in perdition's name, did you make me drink?'

'You must have the weakest head in Christendom, child, if three glasses of French wine can muddle it. Come, the reckoning is paid, and a long one, for that Irishman drinks like a fish; we can settle between us by-and-by. *Allons!*'

He slipped his arm through mine, and led me from the house. The feeble street-lamps swam before my eyes, and I could hardly have walked without my companion's support. Not far from the tavern we found a hackney-coach that had just brought a family-party from the theatre, and this carried us at a good pace to Ranelagh, before the doors of which pleasure-place we alighted.

Here all was confusion and riot—torches blazing, chair-men bawling, footmen squabbling, ducal cha-riots stopping the way, and a crowd of finely dressed people going in and out of the lighted doors.

My companion held me tightly by the arm, and it was as much as we could do to keep our places in the crowd. Standing thus, hustled and pushed on every side, we waited for a time that seemed to me very long, but no black-robed mask approached us. Maskers in red and blue and yellow, Great Moguls and Turkish princesses, shepherds and shepherdesses, sailors, sultans, chimney-sweeps, harlequins, Punchinellos, Sir John Falstaffs, and Abel Druggers, passed and pushed us, but she for whom I waited with throbbing heart and burning brain did not appear.

At last I felt myself tapped on the shoulder by some one amongst the crowd behind us, and turning, found myself face to face with two women in black dominoes and masks. One removed her mask instantly, and I recognized Mademoiselle Adolphine.

'Get us to a coach as quick as you can, Mr. Robert,' she entreated hurriedly; 'my young lady is like to swoon herself.—Oh, but I pray you to sustain yourself, mademoiselle! The coach is all near, and monsieur will lead us there. Lean you on his arm, mademoiselle, and on me.—And you will tell the coachman where to drive, and follow us in another coach, is it not, monsieur? Ah, what of dangers, what of hazards we have run to rencounter you! Monsieur Lestrange is yonder in waiting for mademoiselle, who has gone away with her aunt to the cloak-room; and Miladi Barbara goes to monsieur to say that mademoiselle is too ill to return to the dance. Word of honour, it is a pretty comedy!' and chattering thus, the French maid hurried and bustled us to the door of a coach, into which she pushed her timid companion, who did indeed seem half-fainting.

I pressed the poor little trembling hand, which clung convulsively to mine.

'Shall I not come with you, Dora?' I asked.

'Great Heaven, no!' the French girl shrieked almost hysterically; 'and if one pursues us, and Monsieur Lestrange came to overtake us,—the beautiful affair! Go you into the other coach, monsieur, with your friend, and tell to our coachman to follow yours. Go, then. Is there the time to lose in follies?' cried Adolphine, as I kissed the little hand that still clung to mine, alas! with but too natural fear.

Philip Hay pulled me from the carriage-door, directed the man where to drive, and thrust me into our coach before I had time to remonstrate.

'Drive like ten thousand devils!' he shouted to our Jarvey, who, no doubt used to such clandestine errands and the double or treble pay attendant on them, whipped his jaded horses into a gallop, and in another minute we were tearing, rattling, jolting eastwards at a pace that shook every bone in our bodies, and precluded any attempt at conversation.

I looked out of the window several times on the journey, to satisfy myself that the other coach was following. I think we could scarce have left Ranelagh an hour when we pulled up in a wretched dirty lane, before the dreary entrance of a tavern, whose dinginess was but just made visible by an oil-lamp hanging over the threshold.

'Is this the house?' I asked with a shudder. 'What a horrid place!'

'Zounds, Bob, what a fool thou art! Does it matter by what gate a man goes to heaven! Quick, man! here are the ladies; there is no time for dawdling. My parson will be drunk or asleep if we're not quick; 'tis an hour after our time.—This way, mademoiselle; support your mistress. The stairs are somewhat rotten, and might be cleaner.—The chapel is an ugly one, miss; but this dirty stair is like Jacob's ladder, for here are seen angels ascending and descending.—Come, Bob.'

He opened a door and ushered us into a chamber lighted with two tallow-candles in brass candlesticks.

These stood on a table covered with a dirty cloth, and surmounted by a greasy, dilapidated-looking prayer-book, upon the cover of which, in tarnished gilding, appeared the arms of one of the colleges. A man dressed in a grimy surplice, and with a red cotton-handkerchief tied round his head in lieu of a wig, was nodding half asleep over an empty bottle; but he was broad awake in a moment at our entrance, saluted us briskly, clapped himself behind the table, opened his book, and began to gabble the marriage-service, as if for a wager.

The irreverence of the whole affair shocked me inexpressibly. Was this, save one, the most solemn of all ceremonials, to be thus rattled over by a drunkard?

'Stop, sir!' I cried; 'let the lady at least remove her mask.'

'*Mais tu es bête!*' roared Philip Hay. '*Veux-tu que tout le monde sache demain ce qui se fait ici ce soir?* The lady will keep her mask; 'tis the custom with people of her rank.—Go on, parson, and let us have none of your clippings of the service. This is a *bonâ-fide* marriage, remember; but you'll be paid as well as if we wanted to play fast and loose by-and-by.'

I took the little hand in mine. It trembled no
longer, but was now icy cold. The parson rattled
on with the service. Mr. Hay stood grinning at us,
with his arms akimbo and his hat on. The bride's
responses were given in a faint murmur that was
almost a sob. The ring was slipped upon the
slender finger, and the ceremonial being concluded,
a greasy book was produced, in which I signed my
name, and the bride after me. As she took the pen,
Mr. Hay gave a loud huzza, which withdrew my
attention from the register. It seemed the signal
for a fresh arrival. The door of an inner room
opened, and a gentleman entered, who took off his
hat and saluted me with a bow of mock ceremony.
This new-comer was Everard Lestrange. His ironi-
cal courtesy, and the sardonic grin upon his hated
face, told me that I was undone. Till this moment
my brain had been dazed and muddled by the stuff
that had been mixed with my drink; but my
enemy's presence sobered me.

'Let me be first to salute the bride,' exclaimed
my lady's stepson. 'You may remove your mask
now, Mistress Ainsleigh, and let your husband im-
print a hymeneal kiss upon the prettiest lips in Christendom.'

She, my wife,—bound to me irrevocably by the ceremonial just gabbled over by a half-drunken parson,—took her mask from her face, and looked at me pleadingly, piteously, tenderly, with her soft brown eyes.

It was my foster-sister, Margery Hawker!

CHAPTER XIII.

'WHAT devil's work is this?' I cried, drawing my sword, and looking towards Everard Lestrange, who stood at some distance from me, and very close to the door, as if anxious to secure a convenient retreat.

' Oh, Robin, they told me 'twas your wish to marry me!'

' And the desperado draws his sword on the prettiest girl in Berks!' exclaimed Everard Lestrange; ' was there ever such a savage?'

'It is upon you that I draw my sword, liar and traitor!' I gasped. ' Your life or mine shall answer for this night's work.'

'I decline to cross swords with a——'

Before the foul word could pass his lips, I sprang towards him with uplifted hand, and should have struck him across the face with my open palm, but for Philip Hay and the parson, who clutched at my arm, and held me off by their united strength.

'What a fire-eater this foundling of my lady's is!' cried Mr. Lestrange with his languid sneer. 'But why all this outcry? The wife we have given you is young and pretty, and 'twould only have served you right if we had tied you to some wrinkled harridan of the town. True, 'tis not the lady to whose hand and fortune your insolence aspired; but it is scarce six months since you swore you were ready to marry this one at a moment's notice, if her father could find her for you.'

'I offered to marry an honest woman,' I answered, 'not your cast-off mistress.'

My foster-sister sank to my feet with a stifled groan. God help us both! I had but hit the mark too well.

'No; 'twas my other mistress you wanted, with twenty-five thousand pounds for her fortune. You were welcome to my mistress—when I had done with her.'

'Devil! Will you fight me in this room—this moment?' I cried huskily.

'No! I will fight you neither here nor elsewhere, neither now nor at any future time, for a reason which I hinted just now, and which you need not force me to state more broadly. You are no mark for a gentleman's weapon.—Hold the fellow tight, Phil Hay; I have but a few words to say, and am gone.'

'Let me go, Hay!' cried I; 'why do you obey that scoundrel?'

'Because he is paid to obey me, as ma'amselle yonder has been paid for her part in the comedy. Do you suppose a man of the world like myself was to be ousted and cheated by your bumpkinship, without trying to turn the tables on you? I saw how you were playing your cards from the day we came to Hauteville. Your father was my father's rival, and it was natural to me to hate you. And you, my lady stepmother's beggarly foundling, must needs come between me and the girl that was betrothed to me. A pretty gentleman indeed to steal my mistress! I saw through your artifices, and when you came to London, took care to place my spy upon your track.'

'What!' I roared, shaking myself free from Philip's grasp.

'Yes, Mr. Simplicity; your chosen friend and boon companion is my led-captain, Mr. Hay, a

gentleman who has been in my service for the last
five years.'

' O God, what a dastardly world ! '

' Forgive me, Bob; thou'rt the best fellow I ever
knew, and I love thee with all my heart,' said Hay,
with a strange softness in his tone ; ' but I am a
scoundrel by profession. 'Tis one of the trades poor
men live by, you see, and men must live.'

' Yes, and vipers too ; they plead their privilege
to crawl and sting. Great God, this is hard ! '

I sank into a chair, touched to the very heart by
this hideous treachery. I had grown fonder of the
man than I thought. As I sat for some moments,
confounded, forgetful of Everard Lestrange, I felt a
little hand thrust gently into mine. It was Margery's.
The wretched girl had not yet risen from the spot
where she had sunk down at my feet.

' Forgive *me*, Robin,' she pleaded ; ' indeed I did
not know it was a trick that was to be played on thee,
or I would have died before I had taken part in it.
He—Everard—told me it was your wish to marry
me; and oh, Robin, I have been cruelly deceived,
and am not so guilty as I seem. I will never trouble
you, dear ; you shall see me no more ; and the
marriage can be undone.'

'Yes,' cried Everard Lestrange; 'by grim death! Pallida mors is the only parson who can cut the knot which my friend yonder has just tied.'

'The bride was married under a false name,' I said.

'Yes; but the true one is in the register.'

I turned eagerly to the greasy volume that lay open upon the table. Yes, there, below my own signature, appeared that of Margaret Hawker. I remembered how my attention had been distracted while the bride was writing.

'The ceremony could not be more binding if it had been performed in Westminster Abbey. Mrs. Margery is as honest a wife as Lady Caroline Fox. Ma'amselle Adolphine will go back to her service the richer for a fifty-pound note, and will carry her young mistress the pleasing intelligence of your marriage.'

'And do you think I will not carry the truth to Miss Hemsley?'

'That will depend on your opportunities. You made an engagement this evening which you may find somewhat inconvenient to you in your character of bridegroom, and which will certainly put a stop to any stolen visits to the ladies in St. James's Square.'

'I made an engagement! What engagement?'

'Sure, 'twas an engagement to serve the honourable Ayst India Company over in Bengal, and a glorious career it is for a courageous young man!' cried a familiar voice close at hand, and Sergeant O'Blagg came into the room, closely followed by a couple of ruffianly-looking fellows in military trousers and dingy ragged shirts, while thιee or four others looked in from the doorway.

Before I could utter so much as one cry of anger or surprise, these two scoundrels had gripped me on either side. What followed was the work of a few moments—a sharp brief struggle for liberty, in which I fought as a man only fights for something dearer than life, striking out right and left, while the hot blood poured over my face from a wound on my head.

I had but just time to see Everard Lestrange and the Frenchwoman rush from the room, dragging Margery with them, while a long piercing shriek from that wretched girl rang out, shrill above the clamour of the rest; the floor seemed to reel beneath my feet, a roaring thunderous noise sounded in my ears, and I knew no more.

I opened my eyes upon the semi-darkness of a

dilapidated garret, where I found myself lying on a dirty mattress of hay or flock. The atmosphere was thickened with tobacco-smoke, and what feeble light there was, came from two small windows in the sloping roof, closely barred, and festooned with cobwebs. It was the most wretched place I had ever seen, and for some time after waking from sleep, or stupor, I knew not whether it was not an underground dungeon in which I found myself prisoner.

I lay for some time but half-awake, staring at the bare walls of my prison with a kind of stupid wonder, as if it had been a strange picture in a book, which I contemplated half-asleep, and nowise concerned in the matter. Then, by slow degrees, came a little more consciousness, and I felt that I was in some remote degree interested in this dreary place, and in this aching mass of flesh and bone lying on a mattress but a little softer than the ground.

I tried to lift up my right arm, but found it powerless, and smarting with some recent wound. On this I raised my left, which moved freely enough, but not without some pain, and felt my head, which was bound with wet rags. After this effort I closed my eyes, and was awakened presently by a faint odour of vinegar and a hand pressing a mug of water to my lips with almost womanly softness.

' Who's that ?' I asked, opening my eyes.

' One who has deserved your scorn and hatred, but will do his best to merit your forgiveness,' answered a familiar voice; and I saw that the face bent over me was Philip Hay's.

' You here !' I cried; ' I don't want your services. I would rather perish of thirst than take a drop of water from the hand of such a traitor. Go to your worthy employer, sir, and claim your reward !'

' I have got it, Bob. When a wise man has done with the tool he has used for his dirty work, he takes care to put it out of the way. Everard Lestrange promised me a hundred pounds—I have his written bond for the sum—for the safe carrying through of last night's work; but, you see, he finds it cheaper to hand me over to the Honourable East India Company. Dead men tell no tales, you know, Bob; and a man shipped for Bengal is as good as dead; for what with war, and fever, and famine, and hardship, 'tis long odds if he ever sees Europe again. Drink the water, Robert, in token of forgiveness. You and I are in the same boat, and it is best we should be friends. I was never your enemy but in the way of business, and plotted against you for hire, just as better men will plot against a king. Say you forgive me, child. We are too miserable to afford ourselves the luxury of resentment. But for my care, it is ten to one if your eyes had ever opened on this wretched place, and if you had not been thrust into a nameless grave by night with scarce a prayer said over your poor clay.'

' I do not thank you for that,' I answered bitterly; ' death would be better than to waken in such a place as this.'

' Alas! I claim no thanks, Bob; I only ask you to believe that I love thee.'

' Is it possible for me to think that, after the way you have used me?'

' It was in my bond, Bob. You have heard of the honour that obtains among thieves. I had pledged myself to carry through this business; and then, there was another inducement—I desperately wanted that hundred pounds. Egad! Bob, I could have sold my own brother for less money. Joseph's brethren did it, you know, and he treated them uncommonly handsomely afterwards. Besides, I was in that reptile's pay.'

' And your liberal Mr. Cave, and your history of the Amazons?'

'All purely mythological as those ladies themselves, Robert. I have done an occasional article for Cave ; and I know his scrub and hackney writer, Samuel Johnson—a man that talks better than Socrates, and is content to toil in a garret for the wages of a hackney-coachman. But the money I spent while I was with thee came from Everard Lestrange.'

'And that account of your life and adventures with which you entertained me was as mythical as the rest, I conclude ?'

'No, 'fore Gad, Bob. I gave you a tolerably true account of myself. My sins there were but of omission. I did not tell you that after leaving Mallandaine's service I became henchman and hanger-on of your kinswoman's amiable stepson, Mr. Lestrange, curse him !'

Here a thought flashed across me.

'And you have pandered to his vices, no doubt, as you did to those of your first patron. You can tell me how my poor little foster-sister was robbed of innocence, and friends and home.'

'In the usual fashion, Bob,' my companion answered, with a sigh. 'It is as common as an old street-ballad. The very staleness of the thing makes it hateful to a man of genius. But your man of genius must keep body and soul together somehow. There were all the old hackneyed promises—intentions honourable, family reasons why secrecy must be preserved—the old worn-out pleas; and the poor child was but too easily deluded. Your modern fine gentleman will swear to a lie with the easiest air in the world. Men have always done these things, you know; but there was a time when they did them with a bad grace, and were liable to be sorry afterwards. Shame and remorse are out of fashion now. Mr. Lestrange carried his prize over to Paris, where he introduced her to seven other spirits worse than himself, if that's possible, and was angry with the poor little thing because she sickened at such company. In short, our Don Juan soon grew tired of your little rustic beauty.

'He would have planted her on an elderly scion of the *haute noblesse,* who wanted something young and fresh and pretty to complete the furniture of his summer pavilion near Choisy le Roi. But against this arrangement the girl rebelled sturdily; and by this time Sir Marcus had begun to urge upon his son the necessity of an immediate marriage with the heiress, who might slip through their fingers at any moment. So Mr. Lestrange hurries back to London, bringing his mistress with him, whom he hides in a shabby lodging hard by Covent Garden ; and being well informed of your movements by my agency, he sees that his case is somewhat desperate, and that only violent measures can serve him. Whereupon he buys over the French maid—a deceitful, abandoned creature, always ripe for treachery—and plans the agreeable plot to which you—and I, worse luck!—have fallen victims.'

'And that forged letter, on the strength of which Sir Marcus was so quick to condemn me ? I make no doubt you could give me some enlightenment on that subject.'

'Well, yes, I have heard of the forged letter. Sir Marcus Lestrange is a diplomatist ; and it is just possible he played into his son's hand. Be sure he never relished the notion of your inheriting the bulk of Lady Barbara's fortune, which it is likely you would have done had father and son not succeeded in blasting your character. They have done their work pretty well this time ; and may congratulate themselves on a rare success.'

'But do you think I shall not tell my own story,

and denounce their hellish stratagems, when I
escape from this place?'

'Yes, friend Bob, *when* you escape from durance.
God grant you and I may live to see the day that
sets us at liberty; but I fear me my hair and yours
too will be white as silver when that day comes.'

'What!' I exclaimed, 'do you mean to say that
in a Christian land, in this free country, of whose
liberty Englishmen boast so loudly, they can make
us as close prisoners as if we were clapped in some
underground cell of the French Bastille, by virtue of
Madame Pompadour's *lettre de cachet?*'

'I mean to say that the crimping sergeant into
whose jaws I introduced you—more shame to me for
a treacherous scoundrel!—will swear to an engagement between both of us, which latter turn of
fortune but serves me fairly for my wickedness.
He will hold us to an engagement never made,
Bob—for the difference between crimping and kidnapping is only a distinction of words—and we
shall be kept in this loathsome hole with the rest
of those unlucky wretches whom you see sprawling
yonder, until the Honourable East India Company
are ready to draft us on board ship secretly somewhere down the river, and keep us close under

hatches till we are out at open sea; and then they will land us among the cobras and tigers, to defend John Company's factories, and fight the yellow-faced Hindoos.'

'But is there no such thing as escape, Phil?' I asked, in a whisper, and with a glance towards one of the small close-barred windows.

'Alas! no, Bob. We are a valuable commodity; and rely on it they keep us in a strong box.'

'What! and we are held in durance within a few hundred yards of Guildhall, and can find no means of communicating with the authorities?'

'Nay, Bob, our gaolers will take care to prevent us. We are here in the very heart of savage London; and not that jungle to which we shall by-and-by be drafted is better stocked with foul creeping reptiles and beasts of prey. Alas! my simple Templar, thou hast heard men talk of Alsatia, but didst not know that in this civilized city there lies a wilderness more dangerous than burning Afric's sands or Asia's pathless mountains, peopled by creatures as deadly, and even more treacherous, than tiger or serpent. Thou hast not heard of the ruined houses of Shoe Lane and Stonecutter Street, and the deeds that are done in

the darkness behind those blank-shuttered windows.
To thee Black Mary's Hole and Copenhagen House
are empty sounds, signifying nothing; but to the
citizen of London those names have a sinister
meaning. All this part of London is dedicated
to infamy and crime; and I know not when the
reforming power shall arise to sweep away these
dens of iniquity. Sure 'twould take another great
fire to purify them, and another plague would be
scarce a calamity if it decimated their inhabitants.'

'But where are we, Phil?' I asked, addressing
him with my accustomed friendliness, and for the
moment forgetting what reason I had to hate him.
I was indeed, as he had said, too wretched to be
very angry. Every other feeling was swallowed up
in the overwhelming thought of my misery.

'In the next house to that where you were
married. It was Mr. Lestrange made his bargain
with the parson, not I. They were lies I told you
about the business. My noble patron made his
plans, and found the crimping sergeant, and you
and I went meek as sheep to the slaughter. We
fought lustily for our lives though, Bob, both of us.
Half a dozen hulking wretches, armed to the teeth,
surrounded us, and when you went down I had my

battle for liberty. But the odds were too many against me; and when I felt my arms pinioned, and the iron rim of a pistol's muzzle unpleasantly cold against my forehead, I threw up the sponge. 'Tis little good wounding a hydra; and I saw more hulking scoundrels lurking in the doorway. I knocked under, luckily without much hurt, and with all my senses about me, while you, poor wretch, lay like a log at my feet. They picked you up, and carried you through a passage and doorway leading from that house into this—I following. I got a glimpse of other rooms as we were led up to this, which is at the top of a somewhat lofty house; and I saw they were full of wretches playing cards, and sprawling on mattresses, and drinking and brawling, by the light of foul-smelling tallow-candles, prisoners like ourselves. Whereby I conclude there is a house full of recruits for the Honourable East India Company's service, waiting till there is a vessel ready on which to draft them. The Company charter ships nowadays; but not long ago they did all their trading on their own bottoms.'

It was quite dark by this time; and I asked my companion how long we had been in this dismal place.

' Something less than eighteen hours. It was last night, or this morning, at two o'clock, that we were taken prisoners. There has been an old hag in and out half a dozen times to see you. They want you to live, you see, for you are of some value alive, and dead there is the trouble of your burial. Folks have a knack of dying under this kind of durance. It is not three months since the good citizens about St. Bride's Churchyard were scandalized by frequent funerals that were performed under cover of night, with maimed rites, and no entry made in the register. 'Twas found on inquiry that the corpses came from a receiving-house for East-India recruits hard by, where a fever had broken out among the unhappy creatures. But this is no cheering talk, Bob, for a sick man.'

' Death is the only cheerful thought you can give me,' I answered bitterly. ' Death ! Sure I am dead already. What can death do more than treachery has done for me?—to cut me off from all I hold dear ; and, alas ! I die dishonoured, and my darling will be told I was a liar and hypocrite, who never loved her, and married another woman, scorning that sweet girl's affection. Death ! 'Tis a thousand times worse than death. It is purgatory, a state of torment dreadful as the inextinguishable fires of hell. Get from the side of my bed, Philip Hay; for the first time I can lift my right arm I shall surely raise it to slay you. 'Tis by your help I lie perishing here.'

'I deserve no better at your hands,' he answered moodily; 'but you will scarcely care to murder a wretch so ready to die. It would be like slaughtering a rotten sheep. What have I to live for more than you, Master Robert? Toil and danger and scanty food, and death from the hand of some tawny heathen. Faith, we are in the same boat; and to fight and throw each other overboard would but be mutual charity!'

I heard a key turn, and the hag, of whom Philip Hay had spoken, came into the room with a candle and our suppers—a tempting banquet of mouldy cheese and coarse bread.

'If you want beer you must pay for it,' she said, with an imbecile grin; and Philip threw her a shilling, for which she brought by-and-by a quart of liquor which my companion declared to be the vilest twopenny he had ever tasted.

'These places are on the model of spong-houses,' he said; 'and if a prisoner has money he is made to bleed pretty freely. The penniless they must feed somehow, to keep life in the bodies which are wanted as food for gunpowder.'

'I have a pocket-book full of notes,' said I; 'would it not be wise to spend them in bribing yonder hag?'

'Be sure you have the money before you talk of spending it. In such dens as these they are apt to be handy at picking a pocket. Your coat and waist-coat lie under your head for a pillow. The money was in your coat-pocket, I suppose?'

Yes, the pocket-book had been there, and it was gone—stolen in the scuffle, no doubt. I bitterly regretted this money, for I could not but believe it might have enabled me to buy over my gaolers to my own interest; but I think I still more regretted the book, which contained those comforting sentences of Scripture and philosophy hastily scribbled by the hand of my benefactress.

'Is it my fate through life to lose everything?' I asked. 'Parents, before I had ever known them; friends and good name, and money and liberty. Did I enter this world doomed to loss and slavery; pre-doomed, because of my father's folly? Are my teeth to be for ever set on edge by the sour grapes he ate?'

Happily—and this amidst such utter misery was the solitary consoling circumstance—I had yet the locket with my lady's portrait and hair, which I had long ago hung round my neck by a stout black ribbon, and had worn faithfully every day of my life.

'Even if you had the money I doubt if it would serve you,' said Phil Hay, seeing me lost in a gloomy despair. 'The crone who waits on us is half an idiot, too foolish to aid you if she had the will. Our gaolers are surly ruffians who would take your money and laugh at you afterwards. 'Tis as well to be spared the anguish of a delusive hope. No, Bob, there is no chance for us but to serve our time out yonder, with the chance of coming back some day, if it is our destiny to escape fever and sword, and famine and shipwreck.'

'What is the period? or is there any fixed period for our slavery?'

'Alack! I know not, friend. Were it the regular service to which we were bound, there are rules I could tell you; but of this irregular trader's Company I can affirm nothing. It is an accursed monopoly, opposed to all laws of justice and common sense; and its members make their own regulations. There was a sturdy endeavour some ten years since to throw open our commerce with the East to all adventurous merchants; but by specious argument and solid bribery, in the shape of a loan to government, the Company got their charter renewed, and have now a pretty sure footing in that distant world for which you and I have our places booked.'

After this I sought no further knowledge. I was weakened by the pain of my wounds, and lay languid, almost apathetic, while Philip Hay watched and nursed me with a tenderness that could not but touch my heart, despite my sense of his late infernal treachery. 'Twas strange to be thus cared for by the man who had destroyed me.

I remained in this half-torpid condition for some days, eating scarce anything, and only nourished by some very vile broth which Phil induced the hag to procure for me on his assertion that I was at death's door, and a little brandy, obtained from the same source, and paid for almost as dear as if it had been melted gold.

Under my companion's care I mended a little, and was able to rise from my wretched pallet, wash and dress myself, and pace feebly to and fro our dreary dungeon—than which I little thought ever to inhabit

a more dismal abode. Then came upon me in all its
intensity the agony of despair; and never in all my
after career did I suffer pangs so keen as those that
rent my heart during my habitation of this loathsome garret. Cut off alive from all I loved, tortured
by the certainty that the woman for whom I would
have given my life must needs believe me the basest
of men, there was no source, save One to which I
had not yet learned to apply myself, whence I could
hope for comfort.

'Dora will believe me a hypocrite and a liar,' I
repeated to myself perpetually; and this one idea
seemed to be the beginning and end of my misery.
My noble benefactress's ill opinion, her bitter disappointment in one she had trusted, I could not yet
bring myself to consider. My dear love, my plighted
wife, forsaken by me without a word, abandoned to
the slow tortures of domestic persecution; it was of
her I thought, and for a long while of her alone.
No, not alone; one lurid image glared red across the
sad picture of my love's despair, and wore the shape
of Everard Lestrange. I had not yet learned to
entreat compassion from the Divine Judge of all
mankind, but daily and nightly did I implore the
vengeance of Heaven on the head of this consum-

mate villain, and that I might be permitted to become the instrument of that almighty wrath. For a meeting with this man, foot to foot and hand to hand, I thirsted with even a more passionate desire than that with which I languished to fling myself at Dora Hemsley's feet and assure her of my fidelity. Alas! not for years were either of these meetings to take place; and here was I, at twenty years of age, prisoner in a garret, with no hope of change except that which would send me forth to eternal exile; yes, eternal; for what were the chances of future distant years to a wretch who hungered for present relief to his immeasurable woes? It was just possible that in the remote future I might be restored to liberty and England; but could I live upon the sorry comfort of such a possibility? And I might come back to find Dora's grave, or to know that she was married and happy, and had forgotten me. It would be the return of a ghost, not a living man—a miserable shadow of past hope and joy restored from the grave to trouble the peace of the living. Great Heaven, what an ingenious torment had Everard Lestrange imagined for the gratification of his malice! To have murdered me would have been a poor revenge compared to this hellish conspiracy, which cut me off

from all that constitutes life, and yet left me to exist
and suffer.

The injuries I had received in the brief skirmish
that followed my wretched wedding were severe, and in
spite of Philip Hay's care of me I suffered a relapse,
and lay prostrate with a low fever, while the garret we
inhabited received several new inmates in the persons
of recruits voluntary and recruits involuntary like
Hay and myself. The former smoked, drank, and
played cards, with much contentment and jollity, the
latter alternately bewailed their fate, cursed their
captors, and joined in the amusements of their
happier companions. Of the land to which we were
destined to travel, most of these had but a vague and
foolish notion. Some confounded the East Indies
with the two Americas, others believed the Great
Mogul still powerful as in the days of Aurungzebe,
and ruler over millions of African negroes. All had
a confused idea that the Indians of Asia scalped their
enemies like the copper-coloured natives of Canada,
that an Englishman single-handed was a match for
about fifty of these Hindoo pagans, that diamond-
mines and temples amply furnished with jewelled
idols, accessible to the greed of any European adventurer, abounded throughout the Oriental continent,

and that gold-dust was the staple of the soil.   Ignorance so complete, or half knowledge so bewildering,
as obtained among these men it would have been almost impossible to conceive, had one not overheard
their conversation ; and I was amazed to find that a
couple of fine gentlemen who had been surprised into
an engagement under the influence of a tavern punch-
bowl were no better informed than the tag-rag and
bobtail that formed the rest of the company.

Utterly helpless though I was, I could not shut
from my mind all idea of escape.   I questioned
Philip Hay upon this subject; but he bade me at
once dismiss so futile a hope from my mind.

' You can't suppose I should omit to reconnoitre
our quarters,' he said.   ' I took my survey before
those fellows came in, and discovered the hopeless-
ness of our case.   If you were strong enough to
climb like a cat—instead of which you can but just
crawl across the room—there would be no chance for
us.   We are here at the top of a lofty house ; below
us a stone-paved yard, amply furnished with spikes,
and in which half a dozen soldier-fellows, with a
stout bulldog for their companion, seem to make
their perpetual abode.   Nor is this all, for as your
own eyes will inform you, our windows are stoutly

barred; and our friends, the recruits who have joined
of their own accord, would no doubt be prompt to
curry favour by giving the alarm and joining against
us in any shindy that might follow. No, Bob; so
long as we remain here, there is nothing for us but
patience and fortitude. They must convey us somehow from here to shipboard, and on that passage
rests our sole hope. If you see any chance of escape
then, snatch it without wasting a moment on consideration; you *can't* easily be worse off than you are,
for once safely shipped, our doom is sealed. And
now keep yourself quiet, Bob, so that you may the
sooner get the better of this foolish fever, which
unfits you for seizing any opportunity that may
offer.'

I did not recover from my fever in time to avail
myself of any chance that might have arisen between
our removal and our shipment, for within a few days
of this conversation we were suddenly aroused in the
dead of the night with a summons to prepare for
our journey. Our preparations were of the briefest,
the wealthiest among us possessing no more than a
bundle; and then, amid hurry and clamour unutterable, we descended the steep dilapidated stair, dimly
lighted by a single oil-lamp, and guarded by Ser-

geant O'Blagg and half a dozen private soldiers. I was barely able to limp downstairs, leaning heavily on Philip's shoulder.

' O Phil!' I cried, as we went down, ' I hope they won't part us.'

Yes, strange as this may seem, in the utter abandonment of my state, I now clung to him who had betrayed me into this misery. In the living grave to which we had both descended, his was the sole familiar face that linked me with the past and assured me of my own identity; and even the sense of this I might well have lost amidst surroundings so strange, and under circumstances so far beyond the limits of every-day experience.

I was thrust with two other invalids, whom I had not encountered until this moment, into a wagon, where we lay helpless upon the straw at the bottom. The wagon was then filled as closely as it could be packed with other recruits, amongst whom I was glad to perceive my betrayer, Philip Hay. Half a dozen sturdy fellows, in military dress, and armed to the teeth, sat at the entrance of the waggon, and kept guard over those within. My late acquaintance, the Irish sergeant, took his post beside the driver, whom he directed; and in this order (the wagon holding in all about twenty people) we rumbled along the deserted streets by many windings and turnings, which led I knew not where. I did, indeed, contrive to lift a corner of the covering of the wagon and peer out into the night, but could distinguish nothing except that the streets were dark and narrow. Chance of escape there was none, had my condition been ever so favourable to the attempt.

After a journey which seemed to me interminable, the wagon came to a stop, and we were taken out in a dreary spot down the river, on the Middlesex shore, and, as I believe, somewhere opposite Greenwich, for I perceived the roofs of many houses backed by rising ground, which I supposed to belong to that place. Here we had but little time for looking around us, but were at once huddled into a boat, like a flock of animals destined for slaughter; and as the rowers' oars dipped slowly into the river, I could but think of that other boat in which we were all of us destined to journey, and that it might be better for most of us were we but shadows hastening to the lower world under the grim convoy of Charon. A little way ahead of us we saw the stern of a large vessel, with lights burning dimly in the faint glimmer of early morning. This ship was our destination. We were handed up the ladder, and conducted to a dismal region called the orlop deck, lighted only by padlocked lanterns, and with no ventilation save from the hatchways. Here we were ordered to shake down as best we might, amidst a company of above a hundred recruits, and an allowance of hot coffee and ship-biscuit was served out to such as had the capacity to eat. I had none, nor any inclination to stir from the spot where I had placed myself. I lay in my hammock staring blankly before me, with such a sense of anguish as was even yet new to me. Until this period I must have hoped, or my present despair could scarce have been so profound. I listened idly to the perpetual tramp of hurrying feet, the roar and clamour of preparation above my head; and yet not quite idly, for I knew that every movement of those eager sailors hastened the ship that was to carry me from all I loved.

The sun rose as the vessel weighed anchor, and the scene on the orlop deck, as the glorious eastern light streamed in upon us through the open hatchways, would need the pencil of Mr. Hogarth to depict. Invalided wretches groaning in their narrow hammocks, or stretched on the bare planks, soldiers and recruits for the most part half-drunk and already bawling for more liquor, while some determined gamblers had contrived to settle to a game of cards, with the top of an empty cask for their table. On every side riot, confusion, squalor, and debauchery; while above us rose the mellow sound of the sailors' voices singing as they weighed the anchor.

'We're off, Bob,' cried Philip Hay, as a loud cheer rang out from the deck. 'Good-bye, mother country, and bad luck to you! No cruel stepdame ever treated her brats worse than you've served me; and I wish you no good at parting, except that you may be rich enough to provide a gallows for one gentleman of my acquaintance. Nay, Bob, cheer up; things mayn't be quite as bad as they seem. There are fortunes to be picked up out yonder by clever fellows, and who knows but you and I may have our chance? We're beginning the world like new-born babes, and it may fall out we have silver spoons in our mouths.'

I turned from him, sick at heart, and buried my face in my meagre blanket, sobbing aloud. Yes, I had hoped until now. I had believed that some event—nay, even a miracle from Heaven itself—must befall to save me from this hapless fate; and now I knew that hope was gone, and Dora, reputation, friends, and country were alike lost to me.

And thus, for the second time, I began the world.

CHAPTER XIV.

MY HONOURABLE MASTERS.

Now followed a passage of my life so long and dreary, a period of such utter and hideous monotony, that the memory of it is rather like the confused recollection of a procession of nightmare-dreams than of an actual experience in this waking world. For ten months our ship ploughed the waters, touching at Madeira, and the Cape, where we were not allowed the privilege of going on shore. For the greater part of a year we wretches lay crowded together in our miserable cavernous abode on the orlop deck— or snatched a brief relief from gloom and suffocation at such times as the captain graciously allowed us to take the air on the booms, or when we took it in turns to share the seamen's watch, but for which respite from the sickening odours of that Gehenna below, we must assuredly have perished. No words can tell how we suffered; and if the helpless

African bondsmen in the middle passage endure more than we did, man's cruelty to his fellow-men is indeed an illimitable quantity. Our quarters were of the closest, our food of the roughest; water was doled out to us by the veriest thimblefuls; the atmosphere we breathed was a compound of foulest stenches; the very pigs and poultry—narrow as was the room allowed them—fared better than we. And this slow torture lasted for ten months.

Brief was the excitement which the sight of land afforded to us; 'twas a bitter, desperate kind of pleasure, a very passion of longing and despair, like that of a lover who snatches one fond look at the mistress who can never be his. To this day I can recall the violent throbbing of my heart as, through the thick haze of evening, Madeira rose upon our larboard bow, and we poor wretches crowded together at the bulwarks and almost fought for a sight of that strange island. 'Twas a month after this that a shoal of dolphins played round the ship; and as these free and happy creatures sported in the sun, I could but remember the legend of Arion, and long for some friendly monster whose scaly back might bear me to the shore. Alas, the days of fable are long gone, and the gods come no more upon earth to rescue man from his fellow-man's oppression!

We had not been long afloat before my fever left me, still very feeble and unlike my former self, but no longer on the sick list. The first business of my convalescence was to obtain the means of writing—which I accomplished with some difficulty, so scant were the accommodations of these dismal quarters. Provided at last with these, I penned a long letter to Lady Barbara, detailing the story of my capture, and describing my present miserable condition. I besought her by the love she had borne my father, by her Christian pity for undeserved misfortune, to attempt my early rescue from a fate so hopeless. I warned this generous friend that the same treachery which had compassed my ruin would blacken my character, and that slanders the most plausible would be invented to rob me of her confidence; and then followed the incoherent entreaties of despair, passionate lamentations, wild messages of affection for the beloved girl I had for ever lost, which, in some small measure, relieved an overcharged heart and brain.

This letter I directed under cover to the milliner in Long Acre, and having secured it, placed the packet in my waistcoat-pocket, in readiness for any homeward-bound vessel with which our captain might exchange greetings. Day after day, week after week, I watched and waited for the friendly sail that was to convey this letter; and my heart sickened as the days wore out, and no vessel came within hail of us. Nor was this all; for on one occasion I endured the sharper agonies of disappointed hope, when, on our captain hailing a trading-vessel, she turned out to be a brig laden with Spanish wine, and bound for the Mauritius.

We had been more than six months afloat when the opportunity I so longed for at last arrived in the shape of a homeward-bound Indiaman, to which the cutter was speedily despatched with a couple of officers. I was not the only one among the recruits eager to send home some greeting; but when I and half a dozen others crowded to the open hatchway and besought the captain to despatch our letters, the kindly gentleman laughed us to scorn. Did we think he could trouble himself with the whims and humours of such dirt? And what had we to write about, pray? Complaints of our treatment, no doubt, which would only make mischief at home, and rob the Honourable East-India Company of good soldiers.

'No,' cried the captain, 'I know what a set of lying, ungrateful rascals you are, and you shall send none of your lies to England by my help.'

This speech the skipper liberally garnished with such blasphemies as were the salt of his daily discourse, and then roared to one of his men to shut down the hatchway and drive that vermin into their holes.

There is no despot so awful as the tyrant who reigns upon his own quarter-deck. Against his cruel will there is no resistance except crime, and to oppose his hellish tyranny is to be at once involved in rebellion and bloodshed. The spark of mutiny is a fire that spreads swift as flame among the parched jungle-grass of the Sunderbunds, and I knew that it would need but little to stir that idle Pandemonium between decks into an active Inferno. Nor was the skipper a person of small importance in the social scale. Eastward of the Cape this Company's captain took precedence of a captain in his Majesty's navy, and he and his brother captains had a seat at the council board, at any of the Presidencies they might happen to be at.

I crept back to my hole with the other vermin, and lay there as desolate as, and more desperate than Job; for I needed no tempter to bid me curse God and die. I think at this time my sufferings had banished all Christian feeling from my mind; and if I endured life when self-murder seemed a relief so easy, it was from no faith in the Divine Providence, no fear of the almighty wrath, but from the one savage hope that, in some time to come, when my cup of anguish had been drained to the very dregs, Fate would give me the opportunity of being revenged on the author of my misery.

After the captain's refusal to send my letter I abandoned myself utterly to despair, and fell into a state scarcely less degraded than that of my companions. Like them, I no longer kept count of the wretched days; like them, I slept a dull dreamless sleep through the dreary nights; like them, I ate and drank the scanty portion given to me with the appetite of some half-savage beast; like them, I forgot the existence of a better world than this floating hell, and blasphemed the God who ruled above that happier earth. And thus the time went past us somehow; in days that had far less of colour and variety than the waves that rolled against our creaking timbers; in nights that were darker than the storm-clouds that brooded over our vessel between the Cape and Ceylon; until one dull stormy morning there rose the cry of land, and a friendly sailor told us that the temple of Juggernaut was visible about fifteen miles to the north-west.

Every creature amongst our luckless herd felt a curiosity to behold this first spectacle which our new country offered us. We crowded to the hatchway, and in the confusion of the moment were suffered to gaze our fill. Dimly discernible to the naked eye appeared the dark outline of a pagoda which, at that distance, seemed not unlike a rude church-tower. Bernier's *Travels* had made me familiar with the monstrous worship that prevails in this temple of the Indian Moloch, the road to which for fifty miles is bestrewn with bleaching bones and rotting carrion, and I felt that the shrine of a religion so ghastly was a fitting object to greet my eyes at the end of this fatal voyage.

'Would to Heaven I could believe in the Brahmin's Paradise, and after steeping my senses in some maddening spirit, cast myself beneath the wheels of the monster god's triumphal car!' I said to myself, as I stood among the squalid crowd, gazing at that dim outline in the distance.

We fancied ourselves now at the end of our journey; but we were doomed to lie within sight of

Juggernaut for two days and nights, and then made but slow head against the swell and current from the north-east. The coast of Orixa is so low as to be indistinguishable from a very short distance, and our sailors were compelled to feel their way by soundings every half-hour. Meanwhile the situation of the herd below was, if possible, a little increased in wretchedness, for the ship was being painted in order to make a fair show in harbour ; and we poor creatures had the worst of the paint, which did much to render an already stifling atmosphere utterly unbearable. Nor did we fare any better by venturing on deck, whence we were driven by execrations from the busy seamen, and had thus no alternative from the misery of our hole below.

I wondered, as I heard the men whistling gaily at their work, to think how brave a thing the vessel would look riding at anchor, and how little any stranger who gazed upon her would suspect the anguish and cruelty that had been suffered between her decks.

On the next day we anchored in Sagor Roads, and the watch upon us being now somewhat relaxed, I crept up to the gun-deck, and from an unoccupied porthole enjoyed a clear view of

Sagor Island—a flat, swampy shore, with tall trees that looked like firs, and beneath them vivid green jungle. Here I saw animals browsing among the swampy grass, and was afterwards informed that these were wild-deer, and that the island is further-more infested by tigers, who will even swim off from the coast to destroy any imprudent boatman who trusts his bark within their ken—whence it is that no bribe will induce the natives to approach this savage wilderness.

While I peered from my porthole at this low-lying island, a dark object floated close beside my post of observation, and drifted slowly past with the tide. It was a human corpse, consigned to the sacred river—perhaps ere death had closed the scene—by the pious hands of its dutiful progeny.

'Alas! poor ghost,' I said, 'art thou the sole friend who dost welcome me to this barbarous shore, where superstition has added her own peculiar hor-rors to the natural terrors of death?'

While we lay at anchor a crowd of boats sur-rounded us, laden with fruit and other merchan-dise, while Sircars—men who practise as agents and money-lenders, and who surpass their fellow-practitioners, the Jews, in the arts of their profession—exercised their fascinations upon the captain and officers of the ship. Now, for the first time, I had the opportunity of observing the living Gentoo, and in his delicately-moulded form and finely-chiselled features I saw much to induce the belief that from this Oriental stock sprang that flower of antique civilization, the Greek.

After lying for some hours at anchor we approached the side of the river opposite Kedgeree, and I beheld a dismal shore, thickly wooded, black, monotonous — the very home of all noxious and fatal creatures, from the tiger and the cobra down to the scorpion and mosquito. Night closed in as I gazed upon this dreary coast, and lightnings flashed incessantly above the fever-haunted woods. The sailors spoke of the place as the grave of all hapless wretches who were doomed to remain many days in its neighbourhood.

At Diamond Harbour we anchored again, and here we recruits were drafted into a smaller vessel sent down from Calcutta for our reception; and on board this we made our voyage up the Hooghly River, a noble stream, across which our vessel tacked as in a sea.

And now the end of our troublous transit had come, or not quite the end, for we were put ashore some miles from the British settlement to which we were bound, and had a weary march through rank woods of Oriental foliage, and afterwards by an ill-made sandy road, scarce worthy the name, with ditches of stagnant water on either side. This being the dry season, we tramped through an intolerable cloud of dust, which, together with the heat, well-nigh stifled us; and so onward, with but brief respite, till we came to one of the ill-guarded gates of Calcutta.

Hence we were marched to the fort, and here we found a very meagre force of mixed soldiery—English, Hindoos, and Topases, so called from the fact of their wearing hats, a species of native Christians, a mixed race, produced by the inter-marriage of natives with the early Portuguese settlers. I had heard and read so much of Oriental magnificence as seen by Jesuit travellers at Delhi and other cities of the East, that I had good reason to be disgusted with the English settlement to which Fate had brought me; but it was yet the humble beginning of British rule, and the con-queror who was to set his foot upon the neck of Indian power, and transform a trading Company into a splendid despotism, was but upon the threshold of his marvellous career. I look back to this period, remembering that it was then I first heard the name of Robert Clive, and can still but wonder at the obscure commencement of that heroic romance of which this young man was destined to be the protagonist. When I landed on the shores of the Hooghly in February, 1751, it was but six years since Clive had arrived at Madras, with no higher hope than belongs to the position of a clerk or writer in the Company's civil service. He came, poor, friendless, and lonely, to the shore of that land which he was fated to hold by a grander power than India had felt since the sceptre of the Moguls slipped from the loosening grasp of Aurungzebe. I, who have drained the bitter cup which stepmother Fortune offers to the lips of friendless youth, can but think with a peculiar sympathy of this unfriended lad, who was sent to India chiefly because his father knew not what to do with him in England, and whose lofty spirit sickened at the common round of daily drudgery, while his warm heart languished in the loneliness of a land so strange.

Nothing could well be more insignificant than Robert Clive's start in life. He whose name was to be in less than ten years the wonder of the civilized

world, and the chief glory of Great Britain, had not
a single friend, nay, scarce an acquaintance, in
Madras, and was of a temper too wayward and
reserved to seek introductions by the common arts
of society. Studious as he was proud, he esteemed
the admission to the Governor's excellent library the
highest privilege he enjoyed. I have been told how
that constitutional melancholy, which was so near
akin to madness, displayed itself even at this early
age, and how one day, on a companion coming into
the young man's room in Writers' Buildings, Clive
begged him to take up a pistol and fire it out of the
window. The man complied. ' Then, by Heaven,
I am reserved for something,' cried Clive; ' for I have
twice snapped that pistol at my head.' Alas, 'twas
but a premature rehearsal of a future tragedy ! *

The fort at Calcutta was ill-defended, and worse
garrisoned. The wide ditch, begun in 1742 by the
Indian inhabitants of the colony, at their own expense, and under a panic-like terror of a Morattoe
invasion, had never been finished. It was designed
to encircle the Company's bounds, and would have
been, when perfect, seven miles in extent; but when
three miles had been completed, after a labour of six

* See Appendix, Note A., at end of Vol. III.

months, the Bengalese, with true Indian supineness, desisted from the work; nor did the Company care for its completion, seeing that no Morattoes had ever been on the western side of the river within sixty miles of Calcutta, and that Allaverdy, the Soubahdar of Bengal and Orixa, exerted himself vigorously to prevent their incursions into the Island of Cossimbuzar.

When I first entered Fort William, I was completely ignorant of the present condition of the country in which I found myself. Hakluyt's voyages and Bernier's pleasant book had made me tolerably familiar with the splendid court and city of the Mahometan conquerors of Hindostan, but of Indian history since the death of Aurungzebe and the decline of the Mogul power I knew scarcely anything; and I cannot but wonder at the small degree of interest which Englishmen at home felt in the adventures of their countrymen in this strange land.

When Philip Hay and I, with the rest of the recruits, reached our destination, we found the meagre garrison of Calcutta commanded by five captains, with corresponding subordinate officers, who agreed in nothing so heartily as their contempt for the station to which they were appointed, and their neglect of all duties connected with it. To drink, to sleep, to gamble, to intrigue with loose-lived native women,

and to absent themselves from their quarters on every
possible occasion, in order to indulge their fancy for
the field-sports of the adjoining country, formed the
rule of their lives. They had indeed sorry inducement for fidelity to their posts. Nothing could be more
dismal than life in the fort, and in the town of Calcutta,
where the few European houses scattered among
the ruder native habitations were in the occupation
of British traders and merchants, who thought of
nothing but the rapid increase of their wealth, or
were absorbed in the discussion of their petty dis-
putes with the Company's committee at home.

And thus did Sergeant O'Blagg's florid promises
of Oriental glory and plunder result in the guardian-
ship of a factory, or storehouse for cotton-stuffs ; and
I found myself at twenty years of age the companion
of a mixed assemblage, and subject to the tyranny
of the Irish sergeant, who proved himself a truculent
scoundrel, before whom the Topases and native soldiers—spahis, or sepoys, as they were called by us—
quailed and trembled.

I have but little need to linger over this portion of
my Indian experiences. My life for the space of one
year was a blank, the monotony of which was broken
only by some petty variety in the details of my suffering. I, whose youth had known only the refined

labours of a scholar, found myself working in a ditch with a mixed gang of British recruits and tawny Hindoos, at some necessary repair of our feeble fortifications, exposed to the glare of a meridian sun in a copper-coloured sky, and threatened with the lash at every symptom of flagging industry.

Our military education meanwhile was of a most primitive order. We shared the drill of the sepoys, who wore their native costume of turban, shirt, and loose cotton trousers, and wielded their native arms of sword and target. The number of our officers was in ridiculous proportion to the pitiful handful of troops, not two hundred in all, and but sixty of these Englishmen, the greater number of my fellow voyagers having been drafted off to Madras. They were too lazy to give us much instruction, too indifferent or unexpectant of danger to be interested in their duty; nor did the seizure and French occupation of Madras, with its loss of millions to the English Company, arouse the garrison of Calcutta to any extraordinary exertion. It appears to me, indeed, that it has ever been a quality of the British mind to await the imminent approach of a peril before taking measures to prevent it; and it was only in the fatal summer of '56 that the five captains of our garrison discovered how ill we were defended.

CHAPTER XV.

DURING my first dismal year at Calcutta, the native magistracy of that presidency was chiefly in the hands of a black Zemindar, or magistrate, one Govindram Metre, who acted as subordinate of the English Zemindar, and deputy during the intervals that frequently occurred between the lapse of one appointment and the commencement of another. It is not to be supposed that a government which depended upon the instructions of a committee at fifteen thousand miles' distance, and was subject to the caprices and often ignorant errors of private individuals, actuated sometimes by private interests, and frequently by private dislikes, could be exempt from abuses; and this frequent change of Zemindars, who rarely held the appointment long enough to learn the least of its arduous and numerous duties, was one of the worst among them.

Before Govindram Metre, all native causes, civil and criminal, were at this particular period adjudged in a tribunal entitled the Court of Cutcherry. In common with most Hindoos, his ruling passion was avarice, and he was only to be propitiated by gifts, while his power extended to the dispensation of the lash, fine, and imprisonment. The luckless wretch who had not so much as a handful of pice to offer as tribute could expect but scanty grace from this functionary; and before the first year of my residence was ended I had seen many among my coloured comrades writhing under the lashes administered by Govindram's subordinates. I had seen a good deal of the Black Zemindar, and had heard many scandals concerning the supposed sources of his reputed wealth, when it was my own ill-fortune to become subject to his tyranny.

The Hindoo year, which commences in April, was not quite three months old, and the summer solstice was still at its height, when I began to suffer from a low fever resembling that which had chained me to my mattress in the Fleet Lane crimping-house. The damp enervating heat of the Bengal climate was in itself enough to cause sickness amongst Europeans, who were compelled to labour without regard to the conditions which only render residence in this country tolerable to the foreigner.   Joined to this, I suffered from inadequate food, miserable lodging, a fitful indulgence in spirituous liquors, that were only agreeable to me because they enabled me for the moment to forget my wretchedness, and a constant depression of mind, unrelieved even by hope : for the letter of appeal which I had contrived to despatch to Lady Barbara soon after my arrival was yet unnoticed.   It is not to be wondered, then, that my health languished and my strength declined. The repairs of the fortifications, trifling as they were, were not yet complete ; for an absolute want of system prevailed at this station, whereby no necessary work was ever finished ; and, ill as I was, I was made to perform my share of the arduous labour—now employed in digging the foundations of a wall, now in wheeling barrows of rubbish for the construction of an earthwork.

I was like to have dropped one day under this work, when Sergeant O'Blagg, who was superintending our labours, attacked me with a sudden fury that for the moment well-nigh took away my breath.

'Look at that rascal, now,' he cried to a young ensign who was lolling beside him on the curtain

above us. 'Did your honour ever see such a lazy
vagabone ?   Oi've had my oi upon him for the last
tree days, and divil a bit harther has he worked than
ye see him now.—Don't dhrag the barrow along like
that, ye scoundrel, but put your showlther to it
with a will, or oi'l know the raison whoy, ye idle
omathawn ! "

For the moment I was too weak to answer
him.

'Don't you see that the lad's ill ?' roared out a
voice from the distance (Philip Hay's), while the
tawny wretches digging near me looked on and
grinned.

'Ill ! yes,' cried the sergeant; 'he shams ill to
skulk his work, the idle beggar, but I'll have none
of his malingering !' and, leaping down from the
curtain, he ran forward as if about to hit me.   But
I had just mustered strength to wheel my barrow
of rubble to the summit of the mound, and the
position of advantage was now mine.   'You un-
conscionable skulk !' roared O'Blagg, shaking his
clenched fist at me; 'this comes of enlisting a
sham gentleman.   I might have known you'd make
no sojer, and never urrun the cost of your passage;
and if it hadn't been to obleege a gentleman who

wanted to be rid of his stepmother's bastard cousin, I——'

He had no opportunity of finishing the sentence, for anger lent me a spurious kind of strength, and I hoisted my barrow of sand and rubbish aloft, and emptied its contents upon the head of my assailant in a suffocating shower.

A dozen fellows seized and dragged me up to the little terrace on the top of the curtain, where the ensign lolled with folded arms, grinning at his subordinate's discomfiture.

My outrage upon my superior was sufficiently obvious. The ensign, who was about my own age, and obviously amused by O'Blagg's stifled execrations and frantic efforts to get rid of the earth and sand that covered his head and shoulders, felt it, nevertheless, his duty to punish me.

'Upon my word this is too bad,' he said very mildly; 'though that fellow O'Blagg deserves to get into trouble with his long Irish tongue. But insubordination of this kind won't do, you see, my lad; and as the captain's out of the way—in point of fact, so uncommonly cut last night that he can't show to-day; and the senior-lieutenant has gone up

the country pig-shooting—I think you'd better take
him to the Black Hole.'

' In irons; ye'll put him in irons, your honour ? '
remonstrated O'Blagg, in a suffocated voice.

' Oh, very well, put him in irons if you like,' cried
the ensign, with a merciful wink to the men, which
plainly meant no irons.

On this I was conveyed to the Black Hole, that
too famous prison, which I was doomed once again
to occupy under circumstances that were to make
that occupation distinguished among the darkest
records of man's cruelty to the end of time.

The dungeon itself was in no manner alarming of
aspect. It was the common prison of the fort, in
which European or native delinquents were indis-
criminately cast for any military misdemeanour.

I found myself in a square chamber of some
twenty feet by eighteen, with two small windows
looking westward, a direction from which no breath
of air is to be expected during this summer season.
To say that the dungeon was somewhat close and
airless in the occupation of one person is perhaps to
be fastidious; but I would gladly have preferred a
more airy apartment for my night's repose; and I
lay down in a corner of my cell with a supreme

distaste for my strange quarters; though Heaven knows the great barrack chamber where I ordinarily spent my nights with the rest of the private soldiers on a wooden platform, was no Sybarite's resting-place.

Great God! could I but have conceived the horrid sufferings that were by-and-by to be endured in that very dungeon, what nightmare-visions must have broken my fitful slumbers, what hideous cries and groans must have sounded upon my sleeping senses, prophetic of agonies to come! But this one exquisite anguish of foreknowledge being spared to mankind, my feverish slumbers were undisturbed by painful dreams.

I was awakened soon after daybreak by a jemmautdaar, or coloured sergeant, who came, attended by a couple of peons, to carry me before the Black Zemindar.

To this I immediately objected, as I had been given to understand that the Court of Cutcherry had no authority over Europeans, and was a supreme tribunal only for the subjects of the Mogul. The jemmautdaar answered with the usual slavish stolidity of these people. He knew nothing except that he had been ordered to convey me before the

Black Zemindar. In vain I remonstrated, and asked to see the captain, or one of the junior officers of my company. The jemmautdaar was bent on executing his orders, which I afterwards discovered he had received from no one but my enemy, Sergeant-major O'Blagg, who enjoyed an extraordinary power in consequence of the prevailing supineness among his superiors.

I was taken to the Cutcherry, and there found myself accused of a murderous outrage upon my superior, with intent to do serious bodily harm; in proof of which, Sergeant O'Blagg showed the somewhat inflamed condition of one eye, which had suffered from the shower of rubbish I had discharged upon my enemy's head.

I had seen something of English courts during my brief residence in London, curiosity having led me to Westminster and the Old Bailey on more than one occasion; but although I had there beheld enough to shock my sense of the sacredness of justice, I was completely unprepared for the flagrant iniquity of a tribunal presided over by an almost irresponsible despot. Enough that I, a subject of His Britannic Majesty King George, was condemned to receive a hundred lashes at the hands of a Gentoo, whose national skill in the administration of this punishment I had heard and seen too much of. The Mahometan abhors our British mode of capital punishment by the gallows, and hanging is therefore forbidden by the Mogul; but, on the other hand, the ruler of Delhi has no objection against his subjects being whipped to death, and the gentoo flagellant will lash his victim with a diabolical dexterity, the exhibition of which would have afforded a new sensation to Nero or Caligula.

The sentence was pronounced, and half-a-dozen black fellows advanced to lay their skinny paws upon my shoulders, in order to convey me to the compound, or open yard, behind the court, where summary justice was to be executed; but as they were in the very act of doing this the sound of a cannon booming across the Ganges arrested them as if spellbound, while a sudden unnatural stillness fell upon the court.

A Hindoo cooley entered in the next moment, and, prostrating himself slavishly before the Zemindar, informed him that a British vessel had arrived off Govindpore, and that Mr. Holwell had just landed, having come on to Fort William in a boat.

I had heard of this Mr. Holwell as a civil servant of some importance in the presidency. He had returned to England between two and three years before, there to end his days, as it was supposed, and nothing could have been more unexpected than his reappearance in Bengal.

My eyes happened to wander towards Govindram Metre at this moment, and never did I see terror more vividly painted upon the human countenance. That dusky change which is more ghastly than pallor, spread itself over his copper-coloured visage; but the man was past-master of all dissimulative arts, and when Mr. Holwell himself, three minutes afterwards, came into the court-house, Govindram Metre received him with florid Oriental compliments and servile smiles.

The Englishman accepted these greetings with exemplary coldness.

'What are you doing here, Govindram?' he asked, looking at me; 'and how comes a dispute between British soldiers to be submitted to the Cutcherry?'

'If it will please the most distinguished and favoured among the deputies of our honourable masters to hear the matter, he will perceive that

it is a case of extraordinary character, which called
for——'

'Not for your interference, Govindram,' interrupted Mr. Holwell. 'This young man is a military servant of the Company, and can only be
punished in accordance with military law.—You
ought to have known better, sergeant, than to bring
your complaints here.'

Mr. O'Blagg, whose importance shrivelled into
nothing before this new arrival, muttered some
excuse.

'Were they going to flog this young soldier?'
asked Mr. Holwell.

The Gentoos assented; and Govindram Metre
began a rambling justification of his proceedings.

'Upon my life, it is shameful!' cried Mr. Holwell
indignantly. 'But it is of a piece with all the rest.
The president is absent at his country-house, and the
five captains of the garrison are asleep under shelter
of their mosquito-curtains, or away at their sports up
the country, and this poor sick lad is brought hither
in order that public justice may be prostituted to
private malice. Why, the young man looks fitter
for a sick-bed than the lash.' And then, turning
to me, he said, 'You are free of this tribunal, but

will have to answer to your captain for your offence against the Sergeant-major. Have you been ill?'

'I have been ill of a low fever for the last three weeks,' I answered; 'but they have made me work all the same, since I have just enough strength to crawl about under threat of the lash.'

'You shall be put upon the sick-list. How long have you been in Bengal?'

'A year, sir. I was kidnapped by the Sergeant-major yonder.'

'Kidnapped! Pshaw! There is no such thing as kidnapping allowed in the Honourable East India Company's service. You mean that you enlisted, and were sorry for it afterwards, and were held to your bond, as all recruits are.'

'I mean that I was betrayed into a house in Fleet Lane, sir, and there detained close prisoner, in company with others, till we were shipped secretly, under cover of night, on board the *Hecate*. I mean that I could not have escaped from that crimping-house but at peril of my life, and that men have lost their lives in the attempt to escape from such houses.'

'Humph!' muttered my new friend; 'you speak as if you were telling truth. I know nothing of

abuses in England.   Abuses here are so many that
the study and investigation of them would occupy
a life as long · as that of Nizam-al-Mulk, lately
deceased at the venerable age of one hundred and
four.'

This was said with a somewhat ominous glance at
Govindram Metre, who gazed upon the newly-arrived
Englishman with upturned eyes, expressive of such
veneration as he might be supposed to entertain
only for the gods of his fathers.

'What is your name, young man ?' asked Mr.
Holwell.

'Robert Ainsleigh.'

'Ainsleigh !   That is a good name, and one I
am bound to honour.   From what branch of the
Ainsleigh family do you come ? '

' My father was Roderick Ainsleigh.   My grandfather was a colonel of dragoons, who married Lord
Hauteville's daughter, Lady Susan Somerton.   I
was brought up at Hauteville, in the county of
Berks; entered at the Temple as a student, and
intended for the law, when it was my ill fortune to
fall in with that kidnapping scoundrel yonder.'

' Not so fast, Mr. Ainsleigh.   You must not call
names, though you do come of a good English

family, and a family that I have reason to respect. If what you tell me be true, I am in duty bound befriend you ; for your grandfather, Colonel Ainsleigh, served with my father in the low countries, and at the bloody battle of Malplaquet, carried him, then a lad, from under the enemy's batteries. So you see, sir, I have to thank your ancestor for my entrance into this world, since, had the French cannon made an end of Ensign Holwell on that famous occasion, there could be no such person as your humble servant.—What say you to this gentleman's story, Sergeant-major ? Did he go by the name of Ainsleigh when you picked him up in London ?'

' Sure he did, your honour ; but divil a bit of an Ainsleigh is he for all that, but the baseborn son of Roderick Ainsleigh, a profligate scamp that got himself stabbed to death in a tavern quarrel ; and my Lady Barbara Lestrange, wife of His Majesty's plenipotentiary to Spain, adopted the young scoundrel and brought him up in charity, and he turned upon her like an ungrateful varmint as he is, and wanted to elope with Sir Marcus Lestrange's niece—a great fortune, and a beauty into the bargain ; but luckily for his family, that he was nothing but a disgrace to, he enlisted himself to me in a drunken fit, whereby the Lestranges got rid of him.'

' If you will let me tell you my story, sir, I think you will believe me,' I said, addressing myself to Mr. Holwell.

'I think I shall, Mr. Robert Ainsleigh,' he answered kindly. ' Your face is hardly the countenance of a liar; and if the blood of my father's friend does but flow in your veins, I care little in what illegal manner you came by it.'

' On my honour, sir, that fellow has no warrant for his foul assertion, except the one fact that the obscurity of my father's death and later days left me without the means of proving my legitimacy.'

After this, Mr. Holwell ordered me to be placed on the sick-list, and I was taken to a somewhat dilapidated building on the outskirts of the fort, that served as an infirmary.

'I will make it all right with your captain,' he said; ' and you, Mr. Sergeant-major, must look over the lad's delinquency on this occasion, to oblige me.'

Mr. O'Blagg replied with extreme obsequiousness, and I began at once to discover what it is to have a friend at court.

The doctor pronounced me suffering from a low intermittent fever, and sorely in need of rest; so I lay at the infirmary for several weeks, during which Mr. Holwell frequently visited me. He questioned me very closely upon the subject of my education, and appeared much surprised to find me possessed of several languages, amongst these Sanscrit—which I owed to the scholarship of my old friend Anthony —and a tolerable proficient in Hindoostanee, the acquirement of which, *vivâ voce* from the native soldiery, and from such meagre books as I could obtain, had been my sole recreation during the last dreary year.

'Why, you are just such a fellow as I want for a clerk and secretary,' he said; 'the young writers they send out are for the most part raw ignorant lads, who are despatched here only because their friends know not what to do with them at home. You have but to improve yourself in Hindoostanee, and to thoroughly master the native character in which their business documents are written, and you would be invaluable to me. Would you like to exchange the military for the civil service, if I could effect such a transfer?'

'To exchange the ignoble slavery I have endured

here for your service would be to pass at once from the depths of Onderah to the Mahah Surgo ; or, in plain English, to exchange hell for heaven.'

'I see you have been studying the Shastah,' said Mr. Holwell, who had already revealed to me that taste for Oriental research which was afterwards usefully displayed in his numerous pamphlets. 'You cannot do better than pursue such studies, for the gentoos will respect you so much the more for being acquainted with the Sanscrit language, the knowledge of which is confined to their Brahmins and learned Pundits. And you would really like to be my secretary, Robert ?'

'Nothing would please me better.'

'I warn you that the work will be of the hardest, and tax your powers of accountancy. I am now engaged in the investigation of a series of frauds committed by that scoundrel, Govindram Metre, which involve the conduct of our finances for the last ten years, and by which that black rascal has pocketed thousands. Do you feel yourself capable of performing the mere mechanical drudgery of such a work ?'

'I feel myself capable of making any endeavour to serve you, sir. I was well drilled into accountancy by my lady's house-steward, who had an old-fashioned veneration for figures; and with a little direction from yourself, I doubt not I should soon master the mysteries of finance.'

Mr. Holwell was contented with this assurance, and set to work immediately to redeem me from my hateful bondage. He was a person of considerable influence in the presidency; and amongst a supine and indifferent community his industrious and energetic habits multiplied that influence tenfold. So, by the time I was sufficiently recovered to leave the infirmary I found myself a free man, and went immediately to Mr. Holwell's house, where I was provided with suitable clothes, a decent chamber, and began life for the second time in the character of a gentleman.

It is not to be supposed I was so base as to forget my companion in misery, Philip Hay, in this happy alteration of my own fate. I tried to enlist Mr. Holwell's sympathy for that reckless scoundrel, and carefully suppressed his share in my betrayal. My new friend promised to do his best to serve my late brother in arms; but he remarked that Mr. Hay bore his lot with supreme equanimity, and was a fellow who would doubtless fall on his feet, tumble from what pinnacle he might.

'We may have some fighting by and by,' said he; 'for at the first hint of a war between the two countries Dupleix will be down upon us here. It is not to be supposed that the French will let us alone for ever after their good luck at Madras. In the event of an attack upon this place, your friend will have an opportunity of distinguishing himself; and be sure the fight would be a desperate one, for while I have a voice to raise in council, the motto of Fort William shall be no surrender.'

I lived to see this promise kept, and against a more cruel foe than the French. I lived to witness the base abandonment of Fort William by its chief military protectors, and its heroic defence by a civilian.

CHAPTER XVI.

I BEGAN my labours as clerk, or secretary, to Mr. Holwell, with a hearty desire to render good service to the one friend I had found on this far foreign shore, and entered at once into the entangled mass of accounts it was my duty to examine.

The Zemindarship is an office of double duties, and involves two separate functions, distinct and almost wholly independent of each other. The Zemindar is not only a judge of the Court of Cutcherry, but he is also superintendent and collector of the East India Company's revenues; and it was in this latter capacity that Govindram Metre, in his post of standing deputy, had enjoyed ample opportunity of amassing a fortune at the Company's expense.

The rapid rotation of the English Zemindarship, which office changed hands two or three times in twelve months, had thrown all the power into this

fellow's hands, since the superior officer, whose
deputy he was, had no time to learn the details of
his office, and little inclination to enter laboriously
into the duties of a position he was to hold for so
brief a period. Mr. Holwell's suspicions of this
man's integrity had been aroused before his voyage
to England, while the attention of the Court of
Directors had also been drawn to sundry depreda-
tions and abuses committed by this official. At the
request of the court, Mr. Holwell had taken pains to
explain the nature of the Zemindarship to the ruling
powers at home; and he now returned invested
with full authority as Zemindar, and not to be
removed from his office without express orders from
England, since no proper investigation of the deputy's
abuses could be possible while the head office fluc-
tuated by rotation as heretofore. Once invested
with full powers, Mr. Holwell spared no labour in
his task of cleansing this Augean stable of foul
accountancy.

It would be but dry work to enter into the details
of Govindram Metre's defalcations. Nothing could
be more iniquitous than his system of embezzlement;
and while the office of Head Zemindar had been a
fluctuating one, nothing could be less liable to detec-

tion, since not one of the natives, from the highest to the lowest, durst with impunity have given umbrage to him, and 'tis they who alone could have explored the dark and intricate mazes in which he had so long concealed his operations from the eye of justice.

Amongst his other functions it was his duty to dispose of the pottahs or leases, which apportioned the Company's farms for the space of one year. These pottahs should have been disposed of by public outcry or auction in the Cutcherry, in the presence of the Zemindar; but instead of being thus offered to public competition, the farms were sold privately at Govindram Metre's own house, at such prices as he chose to assign to them. All the best of these he bought himself, under fictitious names, and immediately resold at a profit of from forty to sixty per cent. This infamous transaction, repeated annually for ten years, and involving several estates, had alone enabled him to amass a large fortune; but this was only one species of fraud amongst many. On the monthly charge of servants, on charges for repairing the Cutcherries or court-houses, for repairing roads, and on other items, this knavish rascal's embezzlements amounted to thousands.

Govindram Metre's summary dismissal from his too profitable office was an act of Mr. Holwell's in which the Court of Directors at home promptly concurred; but the investigation of frauds so complicated, and the exposure of a system of plunder as artful as it was infamous, was a work of years. To discover the Black Zemindar's embezzlements was one thing, to prove them was another and far more arduous labour. Every obstacle by which the genius of dishonesty could hinder the progress of justice was placed in our way by this arch plunderer. A complete retrospective examination of his accounts was impossible, for we were politely informed that the white ants had destroyed some of his papers, while others had been washed away in a great storm. In spite of all opposition on the part of the culprit and his slavish instruments, Mr. Holwell did, however, contrive to lay before the Directors a detailed statement of the frauds to which their property had been subject; while the immediate and remarkable augmentation of the revenues under his charge fully proved that his discoveries were of no hypothetical character. It was reserved for this gentleman in the future to prove how small is the gratitude of princes, or of companies, and to drink to the dregs that cup of neglect so frequently offered to the lips of the faithful public servant.

Before I had been many months an inmate of Mr. Holwell's house, I had the satisfaction of finding that my services were of real value to this kind friend and master. He honoured me with much confidence; and I, for my part, told him my own story without the smallest reservation, save on the one subject of Phil Hay's treachery. Meanwhile, although our life at Calcutta was monotony itself, stirring events were taking place elsewhere; and Major Lawrence, with his brave young subordinate, Robert Clive, was teaching Dupleix that French ambition was not to be for ever unopposed by British enterprise.*

My patron's own numerous duties and high responsibilities kept him employed during all the working hours of the day, and during many weary hours in which no one but himself would have cared to work; while I, stimulated by his example, laboured as unremittingly in my own humbler function. Nor did I confine myself to a clerk's drudgery, for I had taken to heart Mr. Holwell's remarks on the import-

* *See* Appendix, Note B, at end of Vol. III.

ance of an acquaintance with the native language, and I devoted a great deal of my spare time to the study of Persian, Hindostanee, and the vulgar Bengalee, under the tuition of a mild-faced moonshee, who came to my quarters nightly to instruct me in those tongues. With this learned man I read the original Shastah, and its more modern and corrupt versions, and thus became familiar with the theogony of Hindostan, between which and the Greek system, as recorded by Hesiod, I did not fail to find occasional coincidences. It was, indeed, to hard mental labour that I could alone look for distraction from the painful reflections which oppressed me in this early period of my exile. I had now been a year and a half in Bengal, but had received no letter from England, though I had written three times to my benefactress, in each several letter setting forth my griefs with all the persistence of despair. Immediately after my removal from the garrison, I had taken advantage of my liberty to write and despatch two other letters. The first to Mr. Swinfen, of the Temple, to whom I related my sad story in its fullest details, and whom I entreated to take possession of the books and other property I had left in my chambers, amongst which was the Spanish

translation of the *Imitation of Christ*, given to me
by Dorothea Hemsley. I did not, of course, fail to
inform Mr. Swinfen how kind a friend I had found
in Mr. Holwell; nor did I omit to ask his advice
upon the legality of my shameful marriage. My
second letter was addressed to my old guardian and
tutor, Anthony Grimshaw, in whom I scarce doubted
I yet possessed a friend, however foully I might
have been slandered in his hearing. From him I
entreated tidings of those I so fondly loved, and so
cruelly had lost. To him also I gave a full account
of my adventures, for I was determined that if my
wrongs could be righted, the opportunity of righting
them should not be lost by any omission on my part.

Having done this I felt somewhat easier in my mind,
and better able to devote myself to my daily labours.
That was for me a most favourable hour in which my
grandfather, Colonel Ainsleigh, had the good fortune
to rescue Mr. Holwell's father from the enemy's fire,
for I found in this gentleman a constant and affectionate friend. Amply did he repay the debt which
he owed my ancestor. He rescued me from a living
death, far worse than the swift annihilation of a
cannon ball, and taught me to hope when every
circumstance of my life tempted me to despair.

'Your moonshee gives me a most glowing account of your progress, Bob,' he said to me one day, after I had been six months an inhabitant of his house. 'That old bookworm house-steward, of whom you tell me, seems to have grounded you admirably in Sanscrit, and you have, I think, a natural talent for languages. Rely on it, that a familiarity with the native tongues is the safest stepping-stone to success in this country, and the young Englishmen who neglect such studies are stone-blind to their own interests. Dupleix has profited greatly by the assistance of his Creole wife, who was born and educated in Bengal, and whose familiarity with the language and usages of the people, to say nothing of her natural talent for diplomacy, has enabled her to aid and abet him in all his Oriental intrigues. The day will perhaps come when you will have reason to bless Providence for your forced voyage to the East. The stagnation of affairs in this presidency is but a false calm. Be sure we shall have stirring scenes enough by-and-by, and a hard fight to hold our own. But whatever struggles await us I hope everything from the English spirit when once fairly aroused. The British lion is a beast that sleeps long and soundly, but God help his enemies in the hour of his awakening! The French have been for a long time past trying to show us the road to glory, and I think young Clive is beginning to show them that we are capable of learning the lesson. And now, Robert, I want you to put aside your respectable moonshee for to-night, and come with me to a festival that is to be given by our friend and ally Mr. Omichund, a Gentoo merchant, and one of the most remarkable men in this country.'

'I shall be proud to accompany you, sir: but, pray, in what does Mr. Omichund's chief merit or genius consist?'

'Why, faith, Bob, if the truth must be told, I think his chief gift is that which most rapidly wins a man distinction at home, in our native country, as well as among these unenlightened heathens. He has the true Gentoo genius for money-making, and for the last forty years has devoted all the forces of his mind to that pursuit. Our Company has allowed him to provide more of our investments than any other contractor, and by this indulgence on our part—which is against our own rules—and sundry other privileges, he has become the richest man in the colony. His trade extends to the uttermost limits of Bengal and Behar, and his influence with the officers of Allaverdy's court at Muxadavad is so considerable, that we sometimes stoop to employ him as our mediator when we want to get the ear of the Nabob. Not a very honourable position for John Company, is it, Bob? But I live in hope the day will come when John will no longer prostrate himself with eight members before the Mahometan musnud; but will stand erect and defend his hardly-won privileges at the point of the sword. In the meantime we are about to make a serious change in our trading arrangements, and to retrench Mr. Omichund's privileges in a manner which will, I fear, sorely vex that pious Gentoo's soul. Yet it is but one of the trials which he has a right to expect in this ninth stage of purgation. The truth of the matter is, that we have discovered a very serious decline in the qualities of the merchandise provided by his agency, together with as serious an advance in its price. But the man is useful, and it would be a dangerous thing for us to offend him, for which reason I have accepted his invitation to to-night's nátch. Nothing gratifies these people more than the presence of Europeans at their festivals.'

We were carried to Omichund's house in palanquins. Calcutta, when I first knew it, had been in existence

less than fifty years, and was but a sorry assemblage
of bamboo huts and the curious open shops of the
natives, interspersed with occasional large and sometimes handsome houses belonging to Armenian,
native, and English merchants; while here and there
an insignificant building of painted brick and plaster,
surmounted by three small domes, proclaimed itself
the temple of the Mahometan faith ; but how different from the pompous mosque of St. Sophia, or the
Jumma Musjeed (chief cathedral) of Delhi, with its
rich blending of dark-red sandstone and pure white
marble !   At the corner of a road we passed a mean
and dirty house, round which a crowd of natives were
clamouring, with angry gesticulations and frantic
cries.   This, Mr. Holwell pointed out to me as the
Catwallee, a minor police-court, where petty griev-
ances are redressed, and a kind of rough-and-ready
justice administered.

We arrived presently at the Gentoo merchant's
house, a handsomer edifice than any I had yet seen,
and brilliantly illuminated. A mixed crowd of guests
and lookers-on was congregated at the gates, through
which we pushed our way into a spacious hall or
quadrangular court, occupying the centre of the
house, and surrounded by two galleries with innu-

merable doors opening into small apartments.   The
upper story Mr. Holwell pointed out to me as
devoted to the women of the household, who,
although invisible to us, were watching the entertainment from the covert of their Venetian lattices.
I had afterwards good reason to remember this
upper story, and one of its beautiful inhabitants.

The court, which, like a Sevillian patio, is at ordi-
nary times open to the sky, was for this occasion
roofed in with red cloth, and lighted with countless
lamps.   The white-muslin draperies and rich embroidered costumes of the guests; the necklaces and
aigrettes of rainbow-tinted gems, that flashed in
strange contrast to their tawny skins, and shone only
less brightly than their piercing black eyes; the
crowd of servants, of whom my companion informed
me Mr. Omichund possessed three hundred, and who
were augmented by the retainers brought by his
visitors; the buzzing of many tongues, the confusion of perpetual movement, and the curious inhar-
monious native music,—combined to render the
scene one of dazzling bewilderment to my unaccustomed senses.   This was indeed an introduction to
fairyland, and its novelty, for the moment, carried
me completely out of myself.

Now began the amusement of the evening. A band of public dancing-girls advanced into the centre of the hall, and performed a strange barbaric dance, which had in it few elements of European dancing. Nothing did I ever behold so devoid of loveliness, for while the arms, body, and head were exercised in every variety of contortion, the feet, though constantly moving, never stirred from the same spot. Whatever dramatic story might be told by the performance—and the changeful expression of the dancers' countenances seemed to have some dramatic significance—was beyond my humble faculties, and if it was by such strained movements and monotonous posturings that the daughter of Herodias danced St. John the Baptist's head off his shoulders, I can but deprecate the bad taste of Herod as much as I abhor his cruelty. Both Mr. Holwell and myself grew heartily weary of this exhibition, during which we discovered that the splendour of Omichund's palace did not exempt us from the native scourge of mosquitoes, which venomous insect tormented us throughout the evening.

Immediately upon the conclusion of the dance, the great Gentoo merchant espied us, and advanced to welcome Mr. Holwell with demonstrative respect.

They talked together for some time in Hindoostanee,
and I had ample leisure in which to observe Mr.
Omichund.   He was a man of advanced years, forty
of which he had spent in the harassing pursuit of
wealth.   Time thus employed had left its traces upon
a countenance that had once been handsome, and
which was of the most refined native type.   But in
the expression of that countenance I read only evil.
A crafty nature had set its seal upon every feature of
the Gentoo's face.   While the flexile mouth expressed only meekness and submission, the restless-
ness of the observant eyes belied its amiable tran-
quillity; and in those bright and watchful orbs I
fancied I could discover a latent fierceness that
augured ill for Mr. Omichund's enemies.

He had evidently got wind of the discussions respecting him that had taken place in council, and of
the intention to reduce his privileges, and it was
with reference to this that he shaped his conversation to-night.

'I have been a faithful servant to the Honourable
Company, Mr. Holwell Sahib,' he said, 'and have
stood between my honourable masters and the Nabob's anger many times.   The English do not know
the Nabob as Omichund knows him.   These Ma-

hometans are all false; they are false as lies. With one hand they will sign a treaty, while with the other they invoke Allah's vengeance on the party to the bond. Do not let the Honourable Company trust the Nabob unless they have a friend at the Durbar—an Indian like Omichund, who has spent his life among these Mahometans and knows how to deal with them. The Honourable Company have hidden enemies at the Durbar. The French governor, Dupleix, is very powerful—O, he is great and powerful, like the old Nizam, and has a head like him to plot and plan. Governor Dupleix and Jan Begum, his wife, have their spies everywhere. She writes many letters—clever letters—that win friends for Dupleix and the French; for she knows these Mahometans, but not as Omichund knows them. She has not had forty years of dealings with them, as he has. The French are better liked in Bengal than the English; and if the Honourable Company does not keep a friend at the Durbar, there will be danger, much danger.'

'From what quarter, Omichund?' asked Mr. Holwell quietly.

'From the French, from the old Nabob, and still more from his grand-nephew, Mirza Mahmud, who

will succeed him, and who hates the English.   He
has the heart of a tiger, that young man, with the
courage of a rat, and he loves only evil.   Let the
Honourable Company trust Omichund, and he will
by-and-by show them wonderful things and gain
them great friends.   It is not so sure that Mirza
Mahmud shall succeed to the musnud.'

'Indeed!   And who is the pretender?'

'It is too soon to tell you that.   Omichund knows
many secrets, and has much power.   It will be well
for the Honourable Company if they treat him gene-
rously.   But if they rob me of hard-won privileges
—nay, Sahib, I am not the man to threaten,' said
the merchant, checking himself suddenly, but with
an ominous light in his eyes that was in itself a
threat.

'I know that Omichund also has enemies,' he
went on, in a more tranquil tone, 'enemies who
grudge him the wealth he has earned by prudence
and unremitting toil and faithful service to his honourable masters; and those slanderous tongues
would do him evil with the honourable council.   But
his honourable masters are too wise to listen to such
base whisperers.   They know they have a good friend
in Omichund.'

To this, and much more to the same effect, did Mr. Holwell listen with that inscrutable calm which was one of his finest gifts. He had indeed a rare aptitude for business, and a genius for coping with the difficulties and niceties of a perplexing position.

'I am but an insignificant member of the council, Omichund,' he said at last, 'and have little power to influence its decisions. Rely upon it the Company are grateful for all faithful service, and in anything they may do will be influenced only by conscientious motives. But let me not detain you too long from your Gentoo friends, who will be ill-pleased if you devote all your attention to a single English guest.'

On this our host quitted us, but not without many obeisances and Oriental compliments.

'The old fox has been informed of our intentions with regard to him,' Mr. Holwell observed to me when Omichund had left us, 'and I suspect he means mischief. Nothing could be more unwise than to employ him as we have employed him, except this culminating folly of diminishing his privileges. We suffer the man to become possessed of inordinate power, and choose the moment when he is strongest to offer him mortal offence. Upon

my word Robert, this management of affairs in
Bengal is about the prettiest comedy of errors that
was ever enacted.'

The time came, and but too speedily, when Mr.
Holwell had occasion to denominate the mismanaged
business of Calcutta a tragedy, and not a comedy,
of errors.

Before he could say more to me, we were escorted
to the supper-room, where we found ourselves placed
at one of the highest tables, to partake of a sump-
tuous banquet, amid the hubbub of some five
hundred attendants and the barbaric discords of
Hindoo music.

CHAPTER XVII.

NOT many weeks after my attendance at Omichund's nâtch, the English mail brought me a packet of direful news which made me for a long time indifferent to public affairs, and only able to perform my daily duties in the dullest manner. To the arrival of every British ship I had for more than a year looked forward with passionate hope and expectation, and behold at last the white sail came that was to bring me, not solace, but the final agony of despair—the *coup de grâce* that was to end all the weak struggles of my heart with the annihilation of my last hope. In Lady Barbara's affection I had trusted as in a strong rock of defence from the assaults of affliction. Had she not told me that she would be my friend through all the changes of my life, and that even ill-conduct on my part should not cancel her regard for her dead lover's orphan son?

During the last two bitter years the memory of this promise had been my chief comfort ; and again and again, when the arrival of the English mail had brought me only disappointment, I had said to my-self, 'I will wait. I know that this one friend is true to me, and sooner or later I shall receive some proof of her affection.'

I think I could have existed for years buoyed up by this one hope; but even this was taken from me.

Of the three letters which I so anxiously expected, one only came to me, and that was addressed by the hand of Mr. Swinfen. With the letter came a packet, which I found to contain two numbers of the *Gentle-man's Magazine*, and while tearing open the cover of the letter I had time to wonder why he had sent me these. Alas ! I but too soon learned his motive.

Mr. Swinfen's letter ran as follows :—

'MY DEAR MR. AINSLEIGH,—I was at once sur-prised and shocked by the contents of your letter (per ship *Godolphin*, arrived January 4th, 1753) and the shameful infringement of an Englishman's liberty therein described ; but find myself unhappily powerless to redress your wrongs. The system by which you have suffered is an infamous adaptation of the tactics of the press-gang to the East India Company's service, and I doubt not is an abuse that will continue to flourish, in spite of complaint from its victims. I bade one of my clerks copy the story of your capture—of course carefully suppressing all private details—and sent exemplars to the *Gentleman's Magazine* and another journal, but could not obtain either editor's consent to its insertion. The Directors of the E. I. Company are numerous and wealthy, and these slavish journalists do not care to offend so influential a body. There will, I hope, come a day when the English press will be more enlightened, and a British subject may find a prompt hearing, if not a swift redress, for his wrongs.

'Were your present state as pitiable as the condition in which you found yourself on first arriving at Bengal, I should be inclined to move heaven and earth in the endeavour to procure your release and return to England. But, in all candour, I declare that, to my mind, your position at Calcutta, as the confidential secretary of an influential person such as Mr. Holwell, is far superior to any standing you could hope to obtain at home. Pray cherish this

new patron and benefactor whom a kind Providence
has raised up for you in a land of strangers, and
endeavour by your faithful service to become at once
necessary and valuable to him.

'And now, alas! my dear young friend, I come to
the saddest part of my duty, on the performance
whereof I enter with a pain second only to that
which I know the perusal of this letter will inflict
upon you. A heavy loss and affliction has befallen
a distinguished English family, and has at the same
time deprived you of an affectionate and powerful
friend. I will not enter upon details which you
will find related at large in the obituary of the
Gentleman's Magazine for December last past; I
will tell you only that your kinswoman, Lady
Barbara Lestrange, is no more, having expired of
a ruptured blood-vessel within a month after the
marriage of her step-son, Mr. Everard Lestrange,
to his cousin, Miss Hemsley.

'You will perhaps wonder that so kind a friend as
Lady Barbara should have made no testamentary
arrangement in your behalf, since her estate was large
and I believe subject to her testamentary control.
Having adopted you in infancy, she might naturally
desire to extend her care of you beyond the grave,

so far at least as to secure your manhood from poverty.

'I can only account for this omission from the fact that the lamented lady was cut off suddenly, in the very prime of womanhood, and that women are ever slow to consider the necessity of legal preparation for that uncertain hour which cometh as a thief in the night. The dear lady left no will, and her estate thus devolves entirely upon her husband, Sir Marcus Lestrange, no doubt to the ultimate enrichment of his only son. It is but a new example of that common fate by which one Pactolean stream flows into and augments another, leaving the barren plains of earth unfertilized.

'Lastly, my dear friend, let me reply to your anxious inquiries on the subject of your unhappy marriage. I regret to say that you have been rightly informed: a marrige so contracted is valid, and nothing but death can loosen your bonds. You will see in this fact another reason for your prolonged residence in India, by which you escape all the pains and penalties of your position.

'I have taken measures to secure the books and other property left at your chambers, and will cause them to be forwarded to you at Calcutta on receipt of your letter to that effect. My paper will permit me to say no more than that I am

'Your obedient servant and sincere well-wisher,

'H. SWINFEN.

'TEMPLE,
    'January 30th, 1753.'

I lay for hours stretched upon the floor of my chamber, with Mr. Swinfen's letter crushed in. my clenched hand, sobbing like a child. And I had thought that evil Fortune had shot *all* her arrows at my devoted head, while *this* envenomed dart yet remained in her quiver!

It was dark when I rose from the ground, remembering that I had yet to learn the details of my affliction. I groped for a lamp, and having lighted it, seated myself at my desk, and began to examine the magazines Mr. Swinfen had sent me.

In the record of marriages printed in the number for November, now ten months past, I speedily found the following passage, marked in the margin by the sender :—

'On Tuesday, 11th inst., was solemnized, with much splendour, the marriage of Mr. Everard Lestrange, only son and heir to Sir Marcus Lestrange,

of St. James's Square, London, and Hauteville, Berks
(late plenipotentiary to his Britannic Majesty at the
court of Madrid), to Miss Dorothea Hemsley, a young
lady of fortune, whose beauty and numerous charms of
manner and accomplishment have attracted much attention both at court and in the upper circles during
the last two seasons. Several of the most distinguished members of the Ministry were present at
the ceremonial; and the amiable prime minister
himself honoured the occasion by his presence.
The bride and bridegroom are to pass the fortnight
immediately succeeding their union at Thorpstoke,
in Yorkshire, the seat of a member of Sir Marcus
Lestrange's family. It is pleasant to record a marriage which in its auspicious circumstances recalls
the experience of Arcadian fairy-tale rather than the
harsher precedents of common life. The union of
Mr. Lestrange and his fair cousin is a pure love-
match, the young people having grown up together
in a tender and most perfect sympathy of inclinations and sentiments, under the approving eyes of
their kindred. A violent fit of hysterics which
overtook the bride at the conclusion of the ceremony
testified to the intensity of her emotion. Mr. Lestrange is designed for a diplomatic career, and will,

we believe, be the bearer of despatches to her Imperial Highness the Empress of Russia, with a view to the more satisfactory adjustment of the late subsidiary treaty, for which distinguished mission his elegant manners and agreeable face and figure eminently adapt him.'

To me what a satire lurked beneath the hackneyed scribbler's florid paragraph! Love, sympathy!—yes, such love and sympathy as can exist between the tender lamb and its devourer the wolf; between the helpless transfixed bird and its fatal fascinater the snake.

Amongst the obituary notices in the December number of the same magazine appeared a paragraph of more tragic interest:—

'LADY BARBARA LESTRANGE, only daughter and sole heiress of the late Earl Hauteville, and wife of Sir Marcus Lestrange, late plenipotentiary to the court of Madrid. It is with heartfelt regret that we record the decease of this lady, who expired on Friday, November 19th, at her husband's mansion in St. James's Square. Her death was awfully sudden, and occasioned by the rupture of a blood-vessel; but

Lady Barbara Lestrange's health had for some months given cause of alarm to her friends. She had but sufficient time to bid a hurried farewell to her family, the principal members of which, namely, Sir Marcus Lestrange, his son Mr. Lestrange, and his amiable lady, were with her at the time of the sad event. Lady Barbara Lestrange was born in 1712, and was therefore only forty years of age at the time of her lamented decease. She was remarkable for her beauty among the belles of his Majesty's Court some twenty years ago ; and was distinguished during a long residence at Madrid for the urbanity of her manners, the charm of her conversation, and the unaffected piety of her life. *Nascentes morimur, finisque ab origine pendet.*'

In another part of the same magazine I found the notice of an event which accounted but too sadly for the failure of any reply to my letter from my old friend, Anthony Grimshaw.

' *Burglary and murderous Outrage at Hauteville, Berks, the Seat of the late Lady Barbara Lestrange.*

' On Saturday, the 20th November, a frightful outrage was committed by a gang of ruffians upon the person of Mr. Grimshaw, house-steward in the employment of Sir Marcus Lestrange, who narrowly escaped with his life from their brutal assaults. A party of three masked robbers broke into the noble mansion of Hauteville between eleven and twelve at night, no doubt with evil intent upon the plate-room, which is situated in a stone vault under the hall. They seem, however, to have made their entry at an upper window, as it was in an apartment on the first floor—the morning-room of Lady Barbara Lestrange—that Mr. Grimshaw appears to have encountered them. What occurred between the armed ruffians and this unfortunate gentleman is known but to himself, and he is in no condition to relate the circumstances of the encounter. But there are ample evidences that the struggle was a desperate one. A valuable Chinese cabinet of inlaid ebony and ivory was found shattered into a thousand pieces, while the steward lay to all appearance lifeless beside it, his skull cruelly battered by some blunt instrument. The villains contrived to escape by leaping from the window to a terrace below, unperceived save by a frightened housemaid, who, not having seen their faces, has no power to describe or identify them. They were

happily disappointed of their hopes of booty, nothing being missed except a tray of antique coins
from the broken cabinet, where the burglars no doubt
hoped to discover valuable jewels, or they would
scarcely have made this their first point of attack.
Some faint hopes of Mr. Grimshaw's life are entertained, but it is considered doubtful if he will ever
recover his faculties, as the injuries done are likely
to exercise a permanent ill-effect upon the brain.

'This event happened, by a strange coincidence,
within four-and-twenty hours after the sudden death
of Lady Barbara Lestrange, to whom the mansion
and estate of Hauteville belonged in her own right,
and from whom this noble property devolves to her
husband and sole heir, Sir Marcus Lestrange, the
lamented lady having died intestate.'

'A strange coincidence,' I repeated, brooding over
this passage in the report. 'Was this midnight
attack upon my lady's private room no more
than a coincidence? I have heard her say that
she kept family papers in that very cabinet; and
before she is cold in her coffin that cabinet is
broken open by masked rnffians, who go near to
murder her most faithful servant and my only friend.
And my benefactress dies intestate, without care or

thought for the orphan youth she had adopted ; she, whose carefulness for others revealed itself in the smallest things.   O God! it is a strange and wicked world ; and I know not whether the treachery of Mahometan revolutionaries in this Eastern hemisphere is much darker than the plots and stratagems of so-called Christians at home!'

END OF VOL. I.

Printed by Carl Ringer, Berlin.